Henry Edward Manning

The four great evils of the day

Henry Edward Manning

The four great evils of the day

ISBN/EAN: 9783743657939

Printed in Europe, USA, Canada, Australia, Japan

Cover: Foto ©Andreas Hilbeck / pixelio.de

More available books at **www.hansebooks.com**

THE

FOUR GREAT EVILS OF THE DAY.

BY

HENRY EDWARD,

ARCHBISHOP OF WESTMINSTER.

LONDON:

BURNS, OATES, AND COMPANY,

17, 18 Portman Street and 63 Paternoster Row.

1871.

LONDON:

ROBSON AND SONS, PRINTERS, PANCRAS ROAD, N.W.

THE four following Lectures are now printed, in compliance with the request of many who desired their publication. They are printed as they were taken down, with only such corrections as were necessary for the sake of clearness.

CONTENTS.

LECTURE I.

THE REVOLT OF THE INTELLECT AGAINST GOD.

——— ———

' But yet the Son of Man, when He cometh, shall He find, think you, faith on earth ?' St. Luke xviii. 8.

BY this question our Divine Lord intends us to understand that, when He comes, He shall find many who do not believe, many who have fallen from the faith. It foretells that there shall be apostasies ; and if apostasies, therefore that He shall still find the truth; but He will find also those that have fallen from it. And this is what the Holy Ghost, speaking by the Apostle, has distinctly prophesied. St. Paul says, 'Now the Spirit manifestly saith that, in the last times, some shall depart from the faith, giving heed to spirits of error, and doctrines of devils.'[1] And again, St.

[1] 1 Tim. iv. 1.

B

John says, 'Little children, it is the last hour;
and as you have heard that Antichrist cometh,
even now there are become many Antichrists,
whereby we know that it is the last hour.'[2]   The
meaning therefore of our Lord is this; not that
when He comes He will not find the Church He
founded in all the plenitude of its power, and the
faith He revealed in all the fulness of its doctrine.
'The city seated upon the hill cannot be hid.' The
Holy Catholic Church is the 'light of the world,'
and so shall be to the end.   It can never be separated from its Divine Head in heaven. The Spirit
of Truth, who came on the day of Pentecost, according to our Divine Lord's promise, will abide
with it for ever: therefore when the Son of God
shall come at the end of the world, there shall be
His Church as in the beginning, in the amplitude
of its Divine authority, in the fulness of its Divine
faith, and the immutability of its teaching. He
will find then the light shining in vain in the
midst of many who will be willingly blind; the
teacher in the midst of multitudes, of whom many
will be willingly deaf: they will have eyes, and
see not; and ears, and hear not; and hearts that

---

[2] 1 St. John ii. 18.

will not understand. As it was at His first coming, so shall it be at His second. This, then, is the
plain meaning of our Lord's words.

And now, before I enter upon this subject, I
wish to say a word of a superstition which, strange
to say, pervades those who are willing to believe
but little else. For in its incredulity the human
mind is liable to fall into the greatest of all credu-
lities; and one credulous superstition of these days
is this: That faith and reason are at variance;
that the human reason, by submitting itself to faith,
becomes dwarfed; that faith interferes with the
rights of reason; that it is a violation of its prerogatives, and a diminution of its perfection.
Now I call this a pure superstition; and those
who pride themselves upon being men of illumination and of high intellect, or, as we have heard
lately, in the language of modern Gnosticism,
'men of culture,' are, after all, both credulous
and superstitious.

God, who is the perfect and infinite intelligence—that is, the infinite and perfect reason—
created man to His own likeness, and gave him a
reasonable intelligence, like His own. As the face
in the mirror answers to the face of the beholder,

so the intelligence of man answers to the intelligence of God. It is His own likeness. What, then, is the revelation of faith, but the illumination of the Divine reason poured out upon the reason of man? The revelation of faith is no discovery which the reason of man has made for himself by induction, or by deduction, or by analysis, or by synthesis, or by logical process, or by experimental chemistry. The revelation of faith is a discovery of itself by the Divine Reason, the unveiling of the Divine Intelligence, and the illumination flowing from it cast upon the intelligence of man; and if so, I would ask, how can there be variance or discord? How can the illumination of the faith diminish the stature of the human reason? How can its rights be interfered with? How can its prerogatives be violated? Is not the truth the very reverse of all this? Is it not the fact that the human reason is perfected and elevated above itself by the illumination of faith?

There have been three periods of the human reason in the history of mankind. The first period was when the reason of man wandered alone, without revelation, as we see in the heathen world, and most especially in the two most cul-

tivated races of the heathen world; I mean the
Greek and the Roman. The second period was
that in which the human reason, receiving the
light of revelation, walked under the guidance of
faith; that is to say, by the revelation of God of old
to His prophets, and by His revelation through the
incarnation of His Son in Christianity. Lastly,
there is a period setting in—not for the whole
world, not for the Church of God, but for individuals, races, and nations—of a departure from
faith, in which the human reason will have to
wander once more alone, without guide or certainty; not indeed as it did before, but, as I shall be
compelled hereafter to show, in a worse state, in
a state which is in truth a dwarfing and a degradation of the human intelligence.

The first state, then, in which the reason of man
wandered without revelation was the state of the
heathen world. They had no knowledge of God,
except by an obscured tradition, which came
dimly from the beginning. But the condition of
the human reason under faith is an elevated and
a nobler state. No man can read the Old Testament—the Book of Psalms, the Book of Proverbs,
to say nothing of the prophetical books of the

Old Testament—without perceiving at once that, in the most elaborate literature of Greece and Rome, there is nothing which, for intellectual elevation, refinement, and power, is comparable with them. When we come on to the period of Christianity, I may say, in one word, that the history of the progress and the perfection of the human intellect is the history of Christianity itself; and that Christianity has elevated, cultivated, developed, invigorated, and perfected the human intellect. Apart from all hopes of eternal life, and in its mere effect on this world, upon man as man, as a rational being, faith has been his elevation. Lastly, we come to that period of which it is my purpose now to speak. St. Paul, writing to the Thessalonians, says: ' Be not easily moved from your mind, nor be frighted, neither by spirit, nor by word, nor by epistle, as sent from us, as if the day of the Lord were at hand;' because, he says, that it shall not come ' unless there come a revolt first, and the man of sin be revealed, the son of perdition, who opposeth, and is lifted up above all that is called God, or that is worshipped.'[3]

---

[3] 2 Thess. ii. 2-4.

Now, I am not going to enter into the question of when that day will come; that is not a part of the message committed to me. Neither am I going to enter into an exposition of unfulfilled prophecies about the man of sin. But out of this epistle I take one word and one idea. Before that day comes there shall be 'a revolt.' Now, a revolt means a rebellion, a rising, a casting-off of obedience, and the erection of a self-constituted authority in its place. I will try to bring before you the signs and marks of this rising or revolt of the intellect of men that were once Christians, and to show that the intelligence of Christian nations has, in these last ages, begun to manifest the phenomena and signs of a departure from faith, which, though it can in no way affect the immutability, stability, and imperishable certainty of the revelation of truth, any more than blindness can cloud the sun at noon-day, nevertheless shows that there is a current carrying the minds of men away from faith in Christ and in God into the darkness of unbelief.

1. First of all, there exists at this day, and there has existed for two centuries, a certain number of men—few indeed—who profess themselves to be

Atheists, or not to believe the existence of God.
I am sorry to say we have among us a certain
number of such men who, by their speeches and
writings, profess this, which I must call not only a
blasphemous but a stupid impiety. I call it stupid
for this reason. A man whom Englishmen are fond
of calling the greatest philosophical intellect that
England ever produced, in one of his essays has used
these words. Quoting the Book of Psalms, he says,
' The fool hath *said* in his heart, There is no God.'
It is not said, ' The fool hath *thought* in his heart :'
that is, the fool did say so in his heart, because he hoped there might be no God. He did
not say it in his head, because he knew better.
And this explanation is exactly what the Apostle
has written, speaking of the ancient world: 'The
invisible things of Him, from the creation of the
world, are clearly seen, being understood by the
things that are made : His eternal power also and
divinity : so that they' (that is, the nations who
know not God) 'are inexcusable ;' · for, professing
themselves to be wise, they became fools.'⁴ And he
goes on to explain the reason of it ; ' as they liked
not to have God in their knowledge:' they had no

⁴ Rom. i. 20, 22.

love, no liking for Him; there was no moral sympathy with His perfections of purity, justice, mercy, sanctity, and truth. These things were out of harmony with their degraded nature; and because they had no love to retain this knowledge of a pure and holy God, therefore their intellects were darkened. And yet, notwithstanding all this, even these, who not knowing God, and not glorifying Him as God, worshipped and served the creature more than the Creator, these were not Atheists. So far from it, they were Polytheists: they believed in a multitude of gods. So profoundly rooted in human nature was a belief in God, that when they lost the knowledge of the one only true God, they multiplied for themselves a number of false gods. The human mind was incapable of conceiving the perfection of the one only true God, and it divided the Divine idea into a multitude of gods; but it was so profusely and instinctively filled with the notion of the existence of God, that it multiplied God, instead of rejecting His existence. The heathen world, therefore, is a witness and a testimony to the existence of God. It became superstitious, credulous, anything you will, but atheistic it could not be. Nay, more than

this : even the learned men, the more refined and
the more cultivated, they also did not reject the
notion of God; they became Pantheists, that is to
say, they invested everything with divinity. The
thought of God was so kindred to their nature, it
had such a response in them, their intellect and
their conscience testified with such constant accord
to the reasonableness of believing in God, or in
gods, that they invested all things round about
them with a participation in the Divine nature.
How, then, has it come to pass that men, in these
last times, after receiving the illumination of the
Faith, and knowing ' the only true God, and Jesus
Christ whom He has sent,' knowing Him in His perfections, in His attributes, and by His works and
grace,—that they should have fallen lower, I must
say, than even the heathen world, that they should
have come to deny the very existence of God?

They are, indeed, few in number; but, nevertheless, they are active and full of zeal to propa-
gate their opinions. In France there exists a school
of Atheism which has a few disciples also in England; I mean the Positivist school of philosophy.
The founder of it, Comte, taught that the human
intellect has three periods : the first is the period

of childhood, the second is the period of youth, and the third the period of manhood. Now, it says the period of childhood is the theological period, in which the human reason believes in gods or in God. The second period of the human reason is that which the founder of this school of philosophy calls the metaphysical period; and here is a refinement well worthy of note. He says, when men are men, they give up the superstition of believing in God; nevertheless, they fall into the superstition of believing in cause and effect, in law and principle, that is, in the metaphysical conceptions which are intrinsic through the inevitable action of the human reason. He treats these as superstitions. As the belief in God was a theological superstition, so the belief in cause and effect, and consequence, and principle, and law—all this is a metaphysical superstition. Well, the third state of the human reason, which is the perfect state of manhood, in what does it consist? In believing that which we can see, feel, touch, handle, test, weigh, measure, or analyse by chemistry. We may test the facts, but we must not connect them together. We must not say that one thing follows after another by a law, or is caused by it.

An explosion of fire-damp is not caused by the
candle being carried into the pit; it follows after
the carrying of it into the pit, but it is a metaphysical superstition to believe that it is caused
by it. This is what is called the scientific state
of the human mind. And this scientific state of
the human mind is when, having pushed over the
horizon and out of sight the idea of God, the idea
of cause and effect, of law and principle, and all
mental philosophy, we are reduced to this—that we
may count and number and distinguish the things
we see as phenomena and facts, but we must not
connect them together, we must not form conceptions as to why they follow one upon another.
And this is Science, the perfection of human reason! The immediate result of this, of necessity, is
Atheism. I would ask, Is this the elevation of
the human reason? Does this Philosophy dignify,
or perfect, or exalt, or unfold it, or confer upon it
knowledge greater than it had before? If there
can be anything which dwarfs, and stunts, and
diminishes, and distorts the human reason, it is
this. Atheism, then, is a lower abasement of the
intellect than was ever reached by the heathen
world. More than this, it is a degradation and

distortion of the human intelligence; and in proportion as the human intelligence departs from the knowledge of God, in that same degree it departs from its own perfection. Nevertheless, this school does exist among us; and this is the first form, or rather the worst form, of the revolt of the intellect, because it is the revolt of the intellect from God altogether, from His existence, and from all that He has made known to us by the light of revelation, and even from that which He has made known to us by the light of nature, which is the light of reason.

2. Secondly, there is another and a modified form of this revolt. There are men (and I am sorry to say they are more numerous than the last) who, though they do not reject the existence of God, do nevertheless reject the knowledge of God; that is, they profess to believe in a God, because they see with all mankind (except a few who are isolated and abnormal) that the light of reason, the light of nature itself, obliges a man to believe in a first cause, and that this first cause must be a personal cause, an intelligence, and a will. To doubt of this is, as I said before, to be an anomaly in the rational order of man. But, while these men be-

lieve in a God of nature, nevertheless they reject
the revelation which He has given them of Himself.
And how did they come to this state? Not all at
once. They came by progressive stages; and I
protest that, in what I am about to say, I say it
in a sorrow which I cannot put in words, still
more, without the least tinge of controversy; because the longer I live, and the more I see of the
state of our own country, the less am I disposed
to utter one word which can make wider the
unhappy divisions which exist among those who
still believe in Christianity as a Divine revelation.
Nevertheless, I must tell the truth. The first cause
of Rationalism (that is, the rejection of Christianity
in the present day) was the rejection of the Divine authority of the Church of Jesus Christ three
hundred years ago: and that by a law of produc-
tion so legitimate, by an intellectual law so certain,
that, I think, any one who would give himself sufficient time and apply sufficient industry to follow
the history of unbelief in the last three hundred
years would see it to demonstration. When, three
hundred years back, certain nations in the north
and west of Europe had rejected the authority of
the Church as a Divine teacher, they immediately

began to examine the human evidences upon which the doctrines of Christianity reposed. Christianity can only rest either upon a Divine authority— that is, a Divine basis of certainty—or upon a human and historical basis. Having rejected the Divine authority, or the Divine basis, they had nothing left to them but the human and historical basis; and that human and historical basis was the history of Christianity as found in the inspired books of Holy Scripture and in the works of uninspired writers. They began to apply human reason to criticise, to test, to measure the credibility, both extrinsic and intrinsic, of every article of the Faith. I say, first, the extrinsic credibility; that is, whether it could be historically proved that this or that doctrine was believed in the beginning and has been believed ever since: secondly, the intrinsic credibility; that is to say, whether this or that doctrine was in itself reconcilable with the human reason. And applying this critical test, they rejected doctrine after doctrine. We all know how many fragmentary Christianities sprung from what was called the Reformation, differing from each other; the German form of the Reformation differing from the English, the

English differing from the Scotch, and the Swiss from both. These fragmentary Christianities were so many exhibitions of the criticism of the human reason working out for itself what seemed to be credible or probable as to the original revelation of God.

It was not difficult to foresee that one man would go farther than another, that one would reject more than another; and that one man would begin early in life believing a great deal more than he believed at the end of it, and therefore that all things would be in a perpetual flux of mutation and uncertainty; so that for three hundred years the amount of Christianity that has been believed on this human and critical basis has been perpetually diminishing, and the residuum which is left upon that foundation now is incalculably less than that with which men started three hundred years ago. I hardly like to go into positive proofs of this, for fear of wounding where I desire to leave no wound; but it is only this last week when, in one of the highest places of this realm, evidence was quoted from a most unsuspicious and impartial correspondent, writing from Germany, who declared the state of religious belief in that country to be such that neither Rome nor Luther would recognise it as Christianity. And yet that was a country in which, only three hundred years ago, before the intellectual revolt against the Divine authority of Faith arose, Christianity was once perfect. Of England, I had rather not speak at all. I pray every day of my life for England. I never say the Holy Mass without praying earnestly that light may be poured out over England, and that the eyes of men may be purged of their film, to see that they are contending one with another to the destruction of their common inheritance; and that we may one day be all united again, in the unity of the only Faith as it is in Jesus. This is my prayer, and I desire most earnestly to refrain from saying a word which can cause the least estrangement in any one who hears me.

But is it not undeniable that at this moment Christianity in England is being undermined? Is it not certain that Rationalism in every form, whether speculative and cultivated, or gross and vulgar, is, in every generation that passes, expanding and establishing itself more widely among the people of England? Moreover, I am old enough to know that, forty years ago, men believed more than they believe now, that doctrines were then held as indisputable which are now openly disputed.

The rejection of the Divine authority necessarily throws men upon the only alternative—human criticism applied to Scripture, to antiquity, to Fathers, to history, to Councils, and to the acts. of the Holy See. There is nothing on the face of the earth which the human reason does not claim to subject to itself, to sit in judgment upon, to test as if it were the creation of man, to decide its credibility as if man were the measure of truth, to pronounce upon whether it be Divine or not. The result of this anarchy of criticism is, that multitudes of men have rejected Christianity altogether : men, whom but a few years ago I knew firmly to believe in Christianity, are now, to my certain knowledge, Rationalists. They now believe nothing of Christianity, because, having applied the false principle of human criticism to the matter of Divine revelation, they have logically and consistently carried out the application of a false premiss, to the destruction of Christianity altogether. The premiss is false, its result is logical.

Let us now apply to this subject the teaching of the Syllabus. Two of the errors condemned in it are,

1st. 'That the human reason, without any regard to the revelation of God, is the sole and sufficient judge of truth and of falsehood, of right and of wrong, and is a law of itself and in itself, sufficient for the welfare of individuals and of states.'

2d. 'That the human reason is the source of all the truths of religion.'[5]

In the beginning of the last century, there was a book written called *Christianity as old as the Creation.* I need not tell you that that book contained no Christianity. It denied all supernatural revelation, and professed to show that all truth was in the natural reason of man. If we should desire to see the fruit of these principles, we may go back to the end of the last century. See what Paris was in the year 1793; see what Paris is again in the year 1871. Tell me whether the human reason, without Christianity, is a law of itself, and the sole judge of truth and falsehood, and of right and wrong, and sufficient for the welfare of individuals and of states. It was only

---

[5] Syllabus, Prop. iii. iv.

yesterday I read in a public despatch from Paris,
that the Commune had decreed that all religious
teaching should cease in the schools. We know
that the churches, which a short time ago were
employed for sacred uses, are now political clubs,
in which, in the course of the last ten days, death
was unanimously voted to the chief pastor of that
Christian city. These are the fruits of the rejection of Christianity. Such, then, is the second
step in the revolt of the intellect—the revolt
which begins with the rejection of the Divine
authority of the Church of God, and then goes
on to reject evidences, next to reject doctrines,
and lastly to reject Christianity.

3. The third kind of intellectual revolt, and it is
the last of which I will speak, in respect to those
who are without, is a form of false philosophy,
which in the Syllabus is described as 'moderate'
Rationalism, as compared with that of which we
have been hitherto speaking, which is there called
'absolute' Rationalism. Now the moderate Rationalism consists in this : in the retaining a belief of
Christianity, or the professing to believe it; but
the believing of it only so much as, upon private
criticism and its own judgment, the individual

mind is disposed to retain. But is it not obvious at once that the human reason can only stand related to the revelation of God, either as a critic, or as a disciple in the presence of a Divine Teacher? The moment the human reason begins to criticise, to test, to examine, to retain, or to reject, it has ceased to be a disciple; it has become the critic; it has ceased to be the learner, it has become the judge; and yet find me, if you can, any middle point where the reason of man can stand between the two extremes of submitting to the Divine authority of faith as a disciple, and of criticising the whole revelation of God as a judge. There is nothing between the two. Now this kind of intellectual revolt (I must call it by a hard name, but it is an old one, and used by the Apostles) is heresy. What is the meaning of heresy? It means the choosing for ourselves, as contra-distinguished from the receiving with docility from the lips of a teacher—the choosing for ourselves what we will believe and how much we will believe. St. James says, 'Whosoever shall keep the whole law, but offend in one point, is become guilty of all;'⁶ and that, for this reason: He that

---

⁶ St. James ii. 10.

said, Thou shalt not kill, said also, Thou shalt not
steal; but if I steal my neighbour's goods without taking his life, I violate the Divine authority
which runs through both the commandments. In
the same way, he who shall believe all the articles
of faith, and yet reject one of them, in that rejection rejects the whole Divine authority upon
which all the articles of faith alike depend. This
spirit of criticism begins, as I said before, in the
rejection 'of the principle of Divine authority and
the adoption of private judgment, which is essentially, though at first covertly, a violation of that
Divine authority. The human reason thereby unconsciously assumes to itself to be the test and
the measure of that which is to be believed. For
instance; in interpreting Holy Scripture, if I inter-
pret the Book according to the light of my individual judgment, the interpretation that I attach
to it is my own. The text may be Divine, but the
interpretation is human. And this must be, wheresoever the Divine authority of the Church is not
recognised as a principle of faith. You know how
the rejection of this Divine authority has shattered
the unity of faith in England. I say this, as I said
before, with sorrow. I do not charge all those who

are out of the unity of the Catholic faith with heresy. The English people are indeed in heresy, but I do not call them heretics. God forbid! They were born into that state of privation. They found themselves disinherited. They have never known their rightful inheritance. They have grown up, believing what has been set before them by parents and by teachers; their state of privation has been caused by the sin of others three hundred years ago, and by no act of rejection of their own. The millions of our people, the children, the unlearned, the simple, the docile, the humble, the wives and mothers and daughters, the great multitude who live lives of prayer and of charity and of mutual kindness, who never had the opportunity of knowing the truth—to call them heretics would be to wound charity. They have never made a perverse election against the truth; and I heartily believe that millions of them, if the light of the Catholic Church were sufficiently before them, would, as multitudes have done in every age, forsake all things to take up their cross and follow their Master.

4. I must now make application of what I have said, more nearly to ourselves. What I am going

to add, I address most especially to those who
are of my flock.

We live in a country which for three hundred
years has been pervaded by a spirit of opposition
to the Catholic Church. Everything round about
us is full of antagonism to the Faith. The whole
literature of this country is written by those who,
sometimes unconsciously, sometimes consciously,
assume an attitude of hostility to it. I say, sometimes unconsciously, because, being born in that
state, they often do so without being aware that
they have received an heirloom of false principles and of false histories respecting the Holy Catholic Church. Without knowing it, they are
perpetually incorporating them with what they
write; so that the greater part of the literature of
this country, which is in the hands of us all, con-
tains a systematic contradiction of that which we
believe. The newspapers, which fill the whole
country, day by day are animated by a spirit
which is against us; and they are filled by details,
and narratives, and correspondence, and they
must forgive me if I say, fables, fictions, fabri-
cations, absurdities—anything that can pander to
the morbid appetite, to the craving for scandals

against Catholic institutions, Catholic priests, Catholic nuns. Only the other day we read attacks against certain nuns in Paris which, for studied but transparent falsehood, were worthy of the Commission of Henry VIII. How is it possible that Catholics can read these things day by day, and their eyes, and imaginations, and hearts receive insensibly no stain from them? They who walk in the sun cannot help being tanned. You go to and fro in the midst of all this literature and all these daily calumnies, you breathe this atmosphere charged with untruths—how is it possible that you should be unaffected by them? Do we not frequently hear Catholics say: 'Am I to believe this?' 'Can I contradict it?' 'If it be not contradicted, there must be some truth in it.' Little by little it gets into the minds of men with, 'I suppose, then, it cannot be denied;' 'Where there is smoke there is fire.' In this way, falsehoods are insinuated. They are either never contradicted, or the contradiction is never published, or if published, hardly seen. The slander has done its work, and the stain remains. We live where Catholics are few, where those who are not Catholics are the great multitude;

we are bound up with them in kindred, in affinity, in friendship, in business, in duty, in society. It is impossible that we should not live amongst them, work with them, and have friendships with them. Charity obliges us to converse with them, and we hear much that certainly does not tend to confirm the faith. There was growing up in the minds of some men a disposition, which, I am happy to say, is nearly cast out again, to diminish and to explain away, to understate and reduce to a minimum that which Catholics ought to believe and to practise. This spirit began in Germany. It says: 'I believe everything which the Church has *defined*. I believe all dogmas; everything which has been defined by a General Council.' This sounds a large and generous profession of faith; but they forget that whatsoever was re-vealed on the day of Pentecost to the Apostles, and by the Apostles preached to the nations of the world, and has descended in the full stream of universal belief and constant tradition, though it has never been defined, is still matter of Divine faith. Thus there are truths of faith which have never been defined; and they have never been defined because they have never been contradicted.

They are not defined because they have not been denied. The definition of the truth is the fortification of the Church against the assaults of unbelief. Some of the greatest truths of revelation are to this day undefined. The infallibility of the Church has never been defined. The infallibility of the Head of the Church was only defined the other day. But the infallibility of the Church, for which every Catholic would lay down his life, has never been defined until now; the infallibility of the Church is at this moment where the infallibility of the Pope was this time last year : an undefined point of Christian revelation, believed by the Christian world, but not yet put in the form of a definition. When, therefore, men said they would only believe dogmas, and definitions by General Councils, they implied, without knowing it, that they would not believe in the infallibility of the Church. But the whole tradition of Christianity comes down to us on the universal testimony and the infallibility of the Church of God; which, whether defined or not, is a matter of Divine faith. I will make application of what I have said when I sum up the argument I am stating. Next, people began to say : ' I can admit that the Head

of the Church has a supreme authority, but that
authority is not without its limits, and the limits
are here and there.' Now who, I ask, can limit
the jurisdiction of a supreme authority? Who can
prescribe the limits of any jurisdiction but one
who in authority is superior to him who holds the
jurisdiction? This spirit of insubordination was
coming in amongst us; it has no existence now,
because the Council of last year struck it dead.
I should have thought that a generous heart, filled
with the love of God, would have desired to know
more and more of Divine truth, and would have
said, 'Let me know everything which God has
revealed, let me have the fullest and the amplest
knowledge,' rather than be jealous and niggardly
in limiting the growth of that knowledge.

5. Lastly, and this is the only other point I will
at present touch on, the effect of such an atmosphere as that we live in, breathing all the day
long the cold air of a country which for three
hundred years has been opposed to the Holy
Catholic Faith, is to produce that which must be
called practical unbelief, even in many who would
lay down their lives for the dogmas of the Faith.
And that practical unbelief is this: their faith re-

sides in their intellect whole and perfect, but it is cold and unenergetic in their life, and it does not govern and mould the character and the will. They get acclimatised to the temperature round about them. You all know how we become acclimatised to a foreign country, how we can learn the habits and the language and the accent of a foreign people. Such is the state of many who intellectually retain their faith, but practically seem not to believe. They become, for instance, unconscious of the Communion of Saints, of the presence of God, of the operation of the unseen world, of the working of the Holy Spirit of God in the Church, and of the personal agency and subtlety of the enemy of truth. I have given these last two examples, because they are the two stealthy and secret approaches whereby the enemy of truth first assails those who sincerely believe. When opening his trenches against the faith of those who never doubted, he begins with the least noise, and under cover.

I will now sum up what I have said. The revolt of the intellect against God is against His existence, or against His revelation, or against His Divine authority. And there are the two

stealthy and incipient forms of intellectual revolt
to which Catholics are tempted; the one of diminishing what they believe to a minimum, the other
in reducing to the least that which they are bound
to submit to in point of authority, or to practise
in point of devotion.

I can make but one application of what has
been said. Two years ago, when the Œcumenical
Council was summoned to meet in Rome, immediately through all European countries, both those
which are within the unity of the Church and
those which are separated from it, there arose a
conspiracy against the Council. Men of the character I have been describing, with those called
'liberal Catholics,' and, strange to say, Christians
of all sects, and Israelites not a few, revolutionists,
rationalists, chiefly out of the Church, but some
within it, professors, declaimers, secret political societies, discontented and fractious minds already
out of harmony with authority and the Church
in all parts of Europe, combined against the Vatican
Council. This general conspiracy strove, by correspondence, and by articles, pamphlets, and newspapers, to avert one thing, which all alike instinctively felt to be fatal to their pretensions. They

all alike feared lest the infallible authority of the
Head of the Church should be defined as a doctrine of faith. An unerring instinct taught them
that such a definition would require of critics the
submission of disciples. They were perfectly right;
so perfectly right, indeed, that those who desired
to see this definition made, desired it for the same
explicit reason for which others opposed it. It
was well known on either side that we were contending for the Divine authority of faith—the
world against it, the Church for it—and that the
axe was laid to the root of the tree. The conflict
was not for this doctrine or that doctrine, nor for a
fragment in detail, but for the Divine certainty of
the whole. Well, that opposition was encouraged,
flattered, countenanced by the favour of governments and diplomatists, statesmen and philoso-
phers. All the newspaper press and the whole
public opinion of the world was united against
the Vatican Council. It tried to write it down, to
make it ridiculous, to hold it up to contempt;
men staked their literary credit and their authority over men upon the issue of the effort to turn
the Vatican Council aside from its purpose, and
to hinder it from doing its work. I am not sur-

prised that no little disappointment should be in
the minds of those who so conspired. I am not
the least surprised at their saying and writing
sharp and bitter things against us; for a more
complete overthrow of a very powerful conspiracy
was never seen. Well, that being over, we next
heard that after publication of the definition, in
every Catholic country, I know not how many
bishops, how many priests, how many professors,
how many learned men, how many of the Catholic
laity, were to rise up to begin a new reformation.
We held our peace; we knew better. The time
was not come. Words do little; events do everything. We waited. What is the result? Every
bishop of the Church of God acknowledges the
authority of that Œcumenical Council. If there
be here and there a priest who does not acknowledge its authority, they may be counted on your
fingers. I do indeed hear of a professor here and
there; but it is not all learned men that are professors, and it is not all professors that are learned
men. Among the bishops and among the priests
of the Church there are many profound theologians who have never sat in a professor's chair.
It is not the habit that makes the monk, nor is it

the title of professor that makes the learned man; and many that have never sat in the chair of a professor are more profoundly learned than many who have; and there are many sitting in those chairs who, to speak with profuse respect, are not learned. If, therefore, I find that in Germany some professors have been making declarations against the Council, that does not surprise, still less alarm, me. It is against this same rational-istic spirit—that is, the pretensions of perverted intellect—that the whole pontificate of Pius IX. has contended. And it was perfectly foreseen, that the moment this intellectual Gnosticism was touched, it would rise; and the rising has been incomparably less than was expected.

There never was a General Council of the Church after which there followed less of contra-diction. After the great Council of Nice, Arianism became a formal heresy which afflicted the Church for centuries. After the Council of Ephesus, Nes-torianism became a formal heresy which is not extinct at this day. After the Council of Con stance, the spirit of national insubordination sowed the seeds of Gallicanism, which was only extin-guished last year in the Vatican Council. After

D

the Council of the Vatican, or at least its first
sessions, it is no surprise that a handful of professors in Germany should rise up against it; and
when I analyse the list and find out who these
professors really are, I am still farther from surprise. There are, I believe, only two professors of
theology; but we find professors of botany, mineralogy, chemistry, anatomy, physic, and of I know
not what. The other day we saw an address
from the University of Rome to an aged and celebrated professor at Munich. Well, there came an
address from the University of Rome; and there
went up a cry of exultation in England, that even
within sight of the windows of the Vatican, Rome
had protested against the Vatican Council. I
have to-day read the names of the men who
signed that address: and I find that they were,
with hardly an exception, men intruded by the
Italian Government since last September, and
that they style themselves professors of botany,
of mineralogy, of chemistry, of surgery, and one
describes himself as professor of Veterinary Pa-
thology.

Before the Council met, a great preacher in
France, whose natural gifts had filled the land

with his fame, in an evil hour lifted up the eloquent voice which God had given him, against
the Vicar of Jesus Christ. Where is he now?
Lost, powerless, unknown.

The venerable professor in Germany—more
learned, indeed, in history sacred and profane,
than either in Christian philosophy or in theology, the founder of a school and the master of
many disciples—through the whole of the Council
exercised his influence with a skill and a boldness
which would have made itself sensibly felt against
any authority which was not Divine. We looked
forward with anxiety to what might be his future
career. I was fully prepared to hear that which
I have heard; and I feared too that his eminent
example might have led astray a multitude of his
disciples. What do I see? Not a bishop, though
many were his disciples. A few priests, and a
handful of professors; and this is all that comes
after the Council of the Vatican. A little momentary agitation, a little transient noise, and a passing sorrow. The Council has extinguished the
last remaining divergence of thought in respect
to faith, to be found among Catholics. It has compacted and consolidated the Divine authority of

the Church in its head, and therefore in the whole
body, both in the active and passive infallibility.
The authority of the Vatican Council is fatal to the
semi-rationalism which had crept within the Church.
The antagonists knew it well, and the Council
knew it likewise when it made that definition.
There never was a time when the faith of the
Catholic Church was more firm, complete, and
universal than at this time.   And if in the course
of ages a revolt of the intellect has carried away
individuals from the Faith, in the course of the
same ages, the manifestations of the Divine authority of the Church in the midst of mankind
have been made more luminous and self-evident
than ever.

LECTURE II.

THE REVOLT OF THE WILL AGAINST GOD.

———

'The wisdom of the flesh is an enemy to God; for it is not subject to the law of God, neither can it be.' Romans viii. 7.

ON looking back at what I have hitherto said, I feel more than ever the difficulty under which I have been, in laying before you a subject which, if it had been treated in detail, with the exactness which a philosophical or a theological argument would require, must have become entirely impossible in such a popular form. But the treating it in a popular form may perhaps lay my statement open to question and to cavil. Between these two difficulties I can only attempt to give a correct outline. I will therefore remind you briefly of what I have said.

I have spoken of the revolt of the intellect
from God as one of the chief evils of these latter
times; and I instanced in proof of it the rise
of Atheism—a negation of the existence of God—
which I then said, and say again, is characteristic
of these latter days; because the earlier ages of
the world were so profusely penetrated with the
traditionary belief in a Divine being, that, though
they fell into Polytheism, Pantheism, and idolatry,
yet into Atheism, as we know it now, they never
fell. The other intellectual evils of these times
are Deism, or the rejection of revelation; heresy,
or the rejection of the Divine voice of the Church,
the jealous and ungenerous limitation of the doc-
trinal authority of the Church, even in those who
believe in the revelation of the Faith; and lastly,
the practical unbelief of lukewarm and heartless
Catholics. These two last being what may be
called the premonitory symptoms of rationalistic
doubt and of final unbelief.

The next subject before us is the revolt of the
will of man from the authority of God. The connection between the two subjects is evident. We
never will anything which we have not first
thought. There is an action of the intellect pre-

ceding every act of the will; for the will that
acts without the previous guidance of the intellect
is an irrational will. It may be the action of a
man, but it is not a human action, because it is
not under the guidance of reason. Therefore,
before every act of the will, there must be an
act of the intellect or reason. The connection
between the last and the present subject is this:
that if the reason or intellect be rightly directed
by the truth, which is the intelligence of God, the
will will be directed according to the law of God.
But if the intellect be perverted or obscured, then
the perversion or the obscurity will descend from
the intellect into the will, and the will will be
likewise perverted or enfeebled. Now the words
which I have taken from St. Paul's Epistle to the
Romans express this truth. He had already said:
'There is now, therefore, no condemnation to them
that are in Christ Jesus, who walk not according
to the flesh,' but according to the Spirit. 'For the
law of the Spirit of life in Christ Jesus hath delivered me from the law of sin and death; for what
the law could not do, in that it was weak through
the flesh, God sending His own Son in the likeness
of sinful flesh and of sin, hath condemned sin in

the flesh; that the justification of the law might
be fulfilled in us, who walk not according to the
flesh, but according to the Spirit. For they that
are according to the flesh, mind the things that
are of the flesh; but they that are according to the
Spirit, mind the things that are of the Spirit. For
the wisdom of the flesh is death : but the wisdom
of the Spirit is life and peace. Because the wisdom of the flesh is an enemy to God; for it is not
subject to the law of God, neither can it be. And
they who are in the flesh cannot please God.'[1]
Now the word 'flesh' here means simply mankind,
human nature, man as he is without God, man as
he is, with the affections, the passions, the intellect, the will, and the three wounds which came
by the fall; that is, ignorance in the intellect,
disorder in the passions, and weakness in the will.
This is what the Apostle calls the 'flesh.' Now,
he says the *wisdom* of the flesh ; and in the Latin
version in one place it is translated 'the prudence
of the flesh;' in another, 'the wisdom of the flesh;'
and in the original Greek it is the 'mind;' that is
to say, the aggregate of affections, passions, and
thoughts acting upon the will, disturbing and per-

---

[1] Rom. viii. 1-8.

verting it. Human nature in its fallen state is declared to be an enemy of God, not subject to the law of God. St. Paul says that it cannot be subject to the law of God, for this reason: so long as it is in that state of disorder, it must be intrinsically opposed to the will of God; for it is unholy, and God is holy; it is false, and God is true; it is unjust, and God is just; and therefore, like as a crooked line cannot be a straight line—and if the line can be straightened, its crookedness has ceased to exist, for crookedness can never be straight—so it is with human nature, unless it is changed, renewed, and elevated. In renewal it puts off its former disorder, which cannot be subject to the law of God. The disorder ceases to exist.

Now, such was not the state of man when God made him in the beginning. Man was created perfect, both in body and soul. The passions and affections were in perfect subjection to his will, and his will to the will of God. From the first moment of his creation he was constituted in a state of grace, and the Spirit of God dwelt in him, illuminating him with the knowledge of God, ordering his affections and passions according to the law of God, and subjecting his will to the will of God; so that there was a supernatural unity and harmony in his soul, and his soul was, as it were, the Kingdom of God within him. Such was the state of man in the beginning; and the wisdom of the flesh then had no existence—the wisdom of the Spirit reigned in him, which is both life and peace. When sin entered, and death by sin, then the wisdom of the flesh developed itself; that is, human nature in its fallen state, deprived by its own sin of the Spirit of God, became darkened, troubled, disordered, unholy. The unity and harmony which existed before, the dominion of the soul over itself, was shattered and destroyed. The rebellion of the passions and affections against the soul at once arose. As soon as the will of man revolted against the will of God, the passions and affections in him, which till then had been subject to him, revolted. He was punished for his revolt against God by an internal revolt against himself.

Now this rebellion of the soul is healed by the redemption of the Precious Blood of Jesus Christ. In the regeneration of the soul by the Sacrament of holy Baptism, the Spirit of God is once more communicated to the nature of man.

God makes the soul His dwelling-place; the order and harmony of the soul begins to be renewed in Him. The wisdom of the Spirit is the mind of one who, being under the guidance and government of the Spirit of God, has subjected his intellect to the truth of God, and his will to the will of God. He is therefore in friendship with Him. St. John and St. James both say that the friendship of this world is enmity against God, because there is an essential enmity between the state of fallen man and God. But when, by regeneration, the will of man is restored to union with God, friendship with God is restored to man. This, then, is the meaning of the Apostle's words. Now, let us make application of them. A rock of crystal resolves itself into a multitude of crystals, every one of which bears the type of the whole. The primitive form pervades the whole block. In like manner, every regenerate soul restored to friendship and union with God, by the indwelling of the Holy Ghost, is compacted in the Body of Christ: 'unto whom coming,' as St. Peter says, 'be you also as living stones built up, a spiritual house.'[2] And as every

[2] 1 St. Peter ii. 4, 5.

stone is shaped and squared and fashioned
and fitted to the place that it is to occupy, so
every Christian soul, built up into the unity of the
Church of Jesus Christ, grows into a temple in
which God dwells by His Spirit. In this kingdom
the will of God is supreme, and the Holy Spirit
perpetually dwells, pervading the Church with
sanctity. The Church incorporates the will of
God, and makes it visible among men. The sins
of individuals notwithstanding, the Church is conformed by its interior subjection to the will of
God, because it is a spiritual society made up of
individuals, called from all races and languages,
compacted and built together in indissoluble unity,
as they subject themselves, one by one, to the
wisdom of the Spirit, Who dwells in the Church
for ever. But the Church has a twofold mission.
The first part of its work—the highest and the
noblest—is the salvation of individual souls, as I
have described. But it has another: the second
part of the mission of the Church to the world is
the sanctification of the civil society of the world,
that is, of the households and families of men; then
of peoples, nations, states, legislatures, kingdoms,
empires, and the whole civil order of mankind.

The Church has had three periods. The first was the period of three hundred years, while it was accomplishing its spiritual mission for the conversion and salvation of individuals, under persecution. The second period began with the cessation of persecution in the conversion of the first emperor, by whom, it may be said, the civil power of the world first paid homage to the Church of God. From that date down to the sixteenth century, the civil society of the world was pervaded by the Christian law, by Christian faith, by Christian unity, by Christian worship. The laws of God became the laws of Christian nations; the laws of the Church were transcribed into the statutes of Christian people; and the civil and spiritual authorities of the world were united together in peace and harmony. There never was a period in history when the world, as such, was so conformed to the will of God as in that period, from the cessation of the last persecution until the sixteenth century. Do not misunderstand me to say that the world had the note of sanctity. No; sanctity is the note of the Church alone. But even the world then acknowledged God and His revelation, the unity of His worship, the unity of His Church,

the supreme authority of faith, and of its laws.
Even the world—the kingdoms and empires of
the world—acknowledged these things; and that
was a time when, howsoever the passions and
affections of man rebelled, yet the public order of
society was Christian, and the wisdom of the flesh
was, at least so far as public laws could reach, in
subjection to the wisdom of the Spirit. I know
that the history of those times is full of outrages,
horrors, violence, and the worst of crimes; nevertheless, I reaffirm what I have said, that in those
ages the world was Christian and society was
Christian. We have now entered into the third
period of the history of the Church. From the sixteenth century downwards to the present time
there has been an undoing of that work which the
Church, for the previous fourteen hundred years,
had been accomplishing; there has been a pulling
down of the whole fabric; a disintegration of the
Christian society; an erasing of Christian laws
from the statute-books of nations; a breaking-up
of the unity of faith, worship, and communion; a
rejection of the spiritual authority of the Church
over men. I am not now entering into any ex-
amination of this, which will fall more naturally

under our next subject; but I am compelled in outline to state it, in order to bring out the subject which is now before us.

I would ask, then, what is it that has been going on for the last three hundred years? A revolt of the will of man from the will of God, as expressed and embodied in the whole work of the Church for the previous fourteen hundred years. When, three hundred years ago, individuals one by one revolted from the authority of the Church, they laid the first seeds of the revolutions which, in these later ages, have separated whole nations from the unity of the Faith. Individuals began the work in the sphere of private judgment, or of their private conscience before God. But that which begins in the private conscience of men one by one, becomes little by little the collective and public opinion of a people, and is at last forced upon governments and legislatures, and changes the public laws in conformity to itself. Now, for the last three hundred years, there has been a continual expunging of the law of Christianity, of the faith and the doctrines of Christianity, from the laws of Christian peoples; so that I may say that at this moment there does not remain one

single people that has not separated itself formally from its old relations of unity with the Christian Church. Many, as in the north and west of
Europe, have formally separated themselves altogether from the unity of the Catholic Church.
Other nations, that remain at least united in faith
and in outward worship, nevertheless have broken
all bonds and relations with it, except in the bare
retaining of dogma and of spiritual discipline.
And now this revolt against the will of God, as
expressed and embodied by His providence in the
work of the fourteen centuries preceding, has received its momentary completion. The people
most favoured among Christian nations, as having
in the midst of them the throne of the Vicar of
Jesus Christ, have revolted, and with a sacrilegious
and violent invasion have usurped the city of
Rome which, from the beginning of Christianity,
has been the centre and the head of the Christian
Church, and, ever since persecution ceased, has
been the visible throne from which the Vicars of
Christ have reigned, by faith and the Divine law,
over the nations of the world.

1. The first mark, then, of these times is lawlessness. This revolt of the will from God is signally

manifested in the rejection of that order of Christian civilisation which the Divine providence has built up in the whole past history of Christendom. St. Paul, in his Epistle to Timothy, says: 'In the last days, shall come on dangerous times. Men shall be lovers of themselves, covetous, haughty, proud, blasphemers, disobedient to parents, ungrateful, wicked, incontinent, traitors, stubborn, puffed-up, and lovers of pleasures more than of God.'[3] 'Evil men and seducers shall grow worse and worse, erring,'[4] and driving the world into error. Now these words are a prophecy of the latter times of the world; and if these be not the latter times, they have at least the marks already upon them. St. Paul also, writing to the Thessalonians, and speaking again of the latter times, says that 'the man of sin,' 'that wicked one, shall be revealed.'[5] Now, I shall not enter into the question of who that wicked one may be; but we can distinctly understand why St. Paul calls him that wicked one. The word in the original is, 'that lawless' one, that is, one who will not recognise any law but his own will, who will pull down and destroy the work of God. Now, if

[3] 2 Tim. iii. 1-4.   [4] Ibid. 13.   [5] 2 Thess. ii. 3, 8.

E

there be any one thing which is a more powerful solvent of the Christian world than another, it is lawlessness, the rejection of law, the rebellion of the human will, the human will making a law to itself, that is, each individual becoming his own legislator, and each legislator making laws at variance with the wills of others, causing perpetual change, universal discord, isolation of man from man, and because isolation, therefore conflict endless and suicidal.

Now, we hear, day by day, the glorification of revolutions. And what are revolutions? They are the violent disintegration of that order which is based upon authority and obedience; or, in other words, they are the extinction of the idea of law and of obligation, the overthrow of the supremacy of law, of the duties of the human conscience and of the human will to law: first to the law of God, for that is the sole foundation and basis of all authority, and then to the civil and political laws of society, which spring from that Divine law and are sanctioned by it. The first and broadest mark that is upon these days, then, is lawlessness.

I should be anticipating what I have to say

hereafter if I were to take for example any particular people or any particular nation; but I think
no man that has read, be it ever so little, of the
modern books upon what is called ' democracy,' of
its gradual and steady advance, its perpetual and
irresistible development, in countries separated
indeed from us by a wide sea, but closely allied
to us by all that acts and reacts upon peoples of
the same origin, will misunderstand my meaning.
This lawlessness shows itself in these three ways :

First, in individuals ; that is to say, men
have ceased to govern their conduct with reference to the laws of God and His Church. Many
have so completely ceased to do this, that any one
who does so is marked as fanatical or bigoted
or a believer. We have come to the days when
in some countries the man who professes faith is
marked for reproach as a clerical, or soft-headed,
or a reactionist. Even in our own country this is
true. You may not meet it, perhaps, in the society in which you live; a certain refinement re-
presses it. But there are classes more outspoken,
where the truth is told more baldly. Fifty years
ago, if a man did not believe in Christianity he
held his peace, not only out of respect for others,

but out of respect for himself. Now, men have no shame to profess infidelity. Then, the masses professed to be what their fathers were. Now, when, out of some hundreds of working men, one was known to go to church, his companions gave him a nickname, and that name was the most sacred Name that was ever heard on earth. The laws of that Divine Person cannot be vivid in the minds of those who could so disclaim their share in Him.

There is, further, a deliberate and legal departure from the Divine law which lies at the very foundation of social life. Christian matrimony is a Sacrament, and creates an indissoluble bond which death alone can loose. Such was the law of England, not only till three hundred years ago, but until fifteen years ago, though by Acts of Parliament it was violated; that is, by privileges, or private laws for private cases, persons were protected from the penalties of the law. The law of Christendom was the law of England down to fifteen years ago, and the bond of marriage was indissoluble. But the indissoluble bond of marriage is the foundation of the domestic life of Christendom. It was out of that principle of au-

thority and order that Christendom arose in its
unity and purity, in the midst of the unimaginable
evils of the heathen world. And in these days a
blow has been struck at this first principle of
Christian homes, which are the foundation of
political society.

Moreover, in the whole civil and political order
there has risen up in the last century a formal
rebellion against authority. About eighty years
ago was published to the world a new gospel for
the political order of men. It has been called 'the
Principles of '89.' Read it for yourselves, and you
will find it full of what is called 'the rights of
man.' But there are two things of which you will
find nothing. First, you will find nothing there about
the rights of God; and surely they ought to have
precedence; and, secondly, you will find nothing
there about the duties of man; but surely men
have duties. When men rise for their rights, forgetting to say a word about their duties, they are
already in rebellion. But again I am anticipating what belongs to our next subject. I cannot,
however, fail to notice, in order to make this point
clear, that we now are hearing of the rights of
women; and if there can be a sign of a society

inverted, and of the moral order of the world re-
versed, it is the putting of woman out of her proper
sphere—the domestic life—where she is sovereign, and the putting her in that sphere where
she ought never to set her foot—the public life
of nations. To put man and woman upon an
equality is not to elevate woman, but to degrade
her. I trust that the womanhood of England—to
say nothing of the Christian conscience which
yet remains — will resist, by a stern moral re-
fusal, the immodesty which would thrust women
from their private life of dignity and supremacy
into the public conflicts of men. This, again, is
a part of the lawlessness of these days, and shows
a decline of the finer instincts of womanhood, and
a loss of that decisive Christian conscience which
can distinguish not only between what is right
and wrong, but between what is dignified and
what is undignified both for women and for men.
This clamour about women's rights may be taken
as one of the most subtle and most certain marks
of a lawlessness of mind which is now invading
society. This, then, is the first example I will
give of lawlessness in general.

2. And, secondly, this lawlessness is invading

the domestic and private life of men in the form of
luxury; and perhaps there is no country which is in
greater danger from this cause than ours. We are
the wealthiest people in the world. The personal
and the national wealth of England is something
incomparable in the history of mankind. I must,
however, bear witness—and it is full of consolation
to know it—that there is still to be found a common
good sense, a firm resisting manliness, in the English
character—and it prevails also in the characters of
some of the women of England—a determination
not to be softened and pampered. Men refuse to
be made effeminate, and women to be self-indulgent. There is, then, something to resist it; and I
hope, for that reason, that the pestilence of luxury
may not prevail over us. But we are in danger lest
our superabundant wealth should create a material
civilisation, so advanced, so refined, and carried out
with such extraordinary subtlety of invention, that
it will need a very strong and firm will not to be
softened by it. There is no doubt that, in dress, in
pleasures, and in amusements, there is an invasion
of luxury in our higher society which is very dangerous, and for this reason: when people have allowed themselves to go up to the brink of all that

is lawful, it is very easy to trespass, and to go over the line that is forbidden. The line between what is lawful and unlawful in such minds is very faint and shadowy; and those who are always walking on the brink of the precipice, will not be long before they go over. The Apostle, speaking of women, says : ' She that liveth in pleasures, is dead while she is living.'[6] The taint of mortality is upon a refined and luxurious life, though on the outside, like the whited sepulchre, it seems unspotted. There is no doubt that the precept of the Apostle is very necessary in our day and in our country. He says: 'All things are lawful to me, but all things are not expedient.'[7] I know I have the liberty ; I may do a multitude of things with perfect safety of conscience ; but I know this—that it might be an example for others, which would be dangerous to them, and it might also be a danger to myself. At all events, it is more generous, it is more in conformity with the example set me by my Divine Lord and Master, to deny myself in many things that are lawful. Apply this to dress, to pleasures, to amusements, to the expenditure you make on yourself, to your domestic and pri-

_____
* 1 Tim. v. 6.   † 1 Cor. vi. 12.

vate life, and you will find a wide field for its application.

3. Once more. The lawlessness of our times is to be found in our profuse worldliness. What is the world but the aggregate of that wisdom of the flesh, which is declared to be an enemy of God? The world always was and always will be at variance with the sanctity, the purity, the justice of God; and therefore St. John says: 'Love not the world, nor the things which are in the world. If any man love the world, the charity of the Father is not in him. For all that is in the world, is the concupiscence of the flesh, and the concupiscence of the eyes, and the pride of life, which is not of the Father, but is of the world.'[8] And the world is upon us all who live in it: its sun shines upon us, we breathe its atmosphere, we are in contact with it, we eat its food, we converse with it all the day long, and happy are we if we are not tainted by it. Now for the forms in which the world presents itself to us. First, in its ambitions. You perhaps will think that ambition belongs only to public life. There is ambition everywhere, ambition in domestic life; in some

* 1 St. John ii. 15, 16.

form or other, ambition in every one. The desire to
strain upward and to strain onward, to possess
more, to be more, to rise, to get into another
place, on another level, on another elevation, to
outstrip neighbours, to be more than they—what
is this but ambition? We recognise it and call
it by its name, when it is in great and noble examples, and we are ashamed of it when it has
manifested itself in the pettiness of our own private life; but it is ambition still. And this ambition of the world corrupts the hearts of multitudes,
because, where this ambition is, a multitude of
passions spring up round about it—envies, jeal-
ousies, rivalries, contentions, bickerings, rash judgments, detraction of neighbours, depreciations,
running down those who are competing with us
and perhaps outstripping us. All this is the lawlessness of the heart. Its passions are not subject to
the law of God, neither, unless it be changed, can
be. These must be cast out as so many unclean
spirits, before the heart can be subject to the law
of God. Another form of worldliness cleaves to the
material interests of men; such as rivalries in business, in trade, in commerce, in the haste to get
rich, in the ravenous buying and selling and bar-

gaining, in the market, on the stock-exchange, in
the bank, in the counting-house; overreaching of
neighbours, gambling speculations, enterprises of
doubtful integrity, in which the conscience is
strained and honour sacrificed; hardness to those
who labour, undue profits made out of the flesh
and blood of those who are scantily paid for toil,
and then, it may be, fraudulent actions with public
ruin, and all coming from what cause? From the
love of money—from that of which the Holy
Ghost thus speaks: 'The desire of money is the
root of all evils; which some coveting after have
erred from the faith, and have entangled themselves in many sorrows.'[9] Such is the end of lawlessness—the passions, not under the government
of holy fear and of justice, tempted all day long
by the spirit of gain, in the hope of laying up and
of being rich in this world; forgetting the warning:
'They that will become rich, fall into temptation,
and into the snare of the devil, and into many
unprofitable and hurtful desires, which drown men
into destruction and perdition.'[10] Now, is there
any country in the world—except, it may be, a
country which has sprung from our own lineage—

[9] 1 Tim. vi. 10.   [10] Ibid. 9.

in which what I have been describing is to be found more dominant and more ruinous than in our own?

And there is still another form of worldliness, which also is a form of lawlessness; that is, the concealing of the law of God and the taking of the laws of the world instead; or, in other words, the fear and worship of the world. The flattery, the adulation, the sycophancy, with which people will wait upon the world to catch its favour, to be admitted into society, to sit at the tables of rich men, to be known as the acquaintance of those who bear titled names, the mean fawning obsequiousness of those who wait upon the world—where this is in a man's heart, he is not the disciple of Jesus Christ. Our Lord Himself has warned us : ' How can you believe, who receive glory one from another, and the glory which is from God alone, you do not seek?'[11] The worship of the world, and the bondage of the world, the fear of losing its favour, or the fear of incurring its ridicule, degrades millions of men who were created to the image of God, and as men, if not as Christians, ought to be ashamed of such meanness. Surely,

[11] St. John v. 44.

if the law of God were in them, as a living and
constraining principle governing their conscience,
it would elevate them above the world and all its
works.

4. One more example of this subtle worldliness may be found where it is least suspected.
It has invaded not only society, it has also invaded religion; it has entered into the sanctuary. In the beginning, Christians worshipped
God in catacombs at the peril of their lives; they
offered the Holy Sacrifice in vaults of the earth,
in damp dark caverns with altars of rough-hewn
stone, and with lamps which hardly gave light;
in hardness, and in austerity, and in poverty.
There was the spirit of martyrdom in those days.
Afterwards, when the peace of the Church began,
the world turned to shine upon it, and the Church
then worshipped God in basilicas in the noonday
sun. Once, as the Fathers said, its vessels were
wood and its priests were gold. Now, its vessels at least were of gold. Heresies and schisms
sprung up in the midst of splendour; men fled
into the deserts, and set up once more altars of
stone and crucifixes of wood, that they might
worship God in the severity and sanctity of

spirit and of truth.   External splendour of worship
is good, but internal truth and reality in the worship of God is better.   It is right, indeed, and according both to the Divine law and to the pattern
of God's own appointment, that the noblest and
the best gifts of human skill and of human wealth
should be consecrated to His honour.   The Christian Church, as soon as it was able to follow the
example of the saints of the Old Law, offered its
costliest and best to the worship of God.   The
murmuring and declaiming that we hear about
the simplicity of worship has in it the spirit of
him who cast up for how much the ointment might
have been sold; not that he cared for the poor.
This carping against the Catholic Church for the
splendour of its worship covers a disposition to
carp against the truth.   No, the Church of God
by its history bears witness that the service of
God in spirit and in truth requires no external
splendour.   It accepts, indeed, all that the art of
man can do in architecture, in painting, in sculp-
ture, in music, because all these come from God
and ought to be consecrated to God.   The warning of the Lord by the prophet rings in the ears
of Christians: 'Is it time for you to dwell in

ceiled houses, and this house lie desolate ?"[12] It is true of us also that the wealth spent upon the private dwellings of men exceeds ten thousand-fold that which is spent upon the honour and worship of God. The Church, therefore, both consecrates all things to God's service, and also sustains the same spirit of austere interior worship as in the beginning; and the Church has in all ages, by its chief Orders, kept up its testimony that the worship of God, in spirit and in truth, does not need external splendour. St. Francis laid down as the law for his children—the most numerous family in the Catholic Church—that upon the altar there should be candlesticks of wood, and that the vestments of the priest should have no silk. You will not misunderstand me, then, when I say that the spirit of the world will often enter into the splendour of the sanctuary, and that the sounds which fill the ear, and the beauty which fills the eye, may take away the heart and the mind. Unless there be the spirit of prayer and union with our Divine Lord in the heart, men may come and go without worshipping God in spirit and in truth. This is one of our most subtle

[12] Aggæus i. 4.

dangers. Satan knows well how to pass off the intellectual simulation of religious opinion for Divine faith; how to pass off imaginative dreamings about the perfections of saints for practical obedience; how to fill men's imaginations with ideas of asceticism while their lives are self-indulgent; and to make even the splendours, sweetness, beauty, and majesty of Catholic worship a fascination of the sense and a distraction of the soul. The tempter is always busy, and nowhere changes himself into an angel of light so easily as in church. Now, I ask, have you been enough on your guard against this? The Catholic Church, lavish as it is in all splendours, because all things are due to Him who is the Giver of all, has sure and deep correctives to recall its children from the mere fascinations of sense by the eye, or the ear, or the imagination, to the presence of God. Where Jesus is present in the Blessed Sacrament, no splendour can easily withdraw the mind from Him; or if any become lukewarm, there is a prompt and strong remedy in the confessional. They who live in spirit and in truth will adore in spirit and in truth, as well in the majesty of a basilica as in the austerity of a catacomb. The interior spirit vivi-

fies all exterior forms. Ceremonies are a mere mask
to the unbelieving and the undevout. They are the
folds of the Divine Presence, the countenance of
the unseen Majesty, to those that believe and love.

5. The last and the only other point on which
I will speak is one which threatens us all, and that
is, compromise. The days in which we live are not
days of firmness. People who still retain a belief
in revelation nevertheless hear so much against
dogma, that they are often tempted to use the
same language, and to disclaim dogmatism. They
hear so much said against asceticism, that they
try to show their freedom from it by a liberty
which is dangerous. But religion without dogma
is not Christianity, and religion without asceticism
is not the religion by which we can be saved. The
religion of Jesus Christ began in the preaching of
John: 'Do penance; for the kingdom of heaven is
at hand.'[13] There can be no repentance without
the mortification of the senses. The times in
which we live are perhaps, of all times since the
beginning of the Church, the least ascetic. The
luxury, the worldliness, the superabundance of all
that is grand and beautiful even in the external

---

[13] St. Matt. iii. 2.

F

worship of the Church, may help to lead men away. The fault indeed is theirs. They can turn anything into temptation; everything will be a snare if they will not correct it by a spirit of obedience to the law of God. Now, there are many marks of this shallow mind among us First, there is little mortification of the intellect: the intellect ranges without check and without limit; men read every book that comes to hand, every newspaper they find on the table. They do not ask whether it is for the Faith, or against the Faith; is it heretical, or is it sound; is it pure, or is it impure. They begin without discrimination; they read on without fear; they find the book to be heretical, erroneous, scandalous, licentious, and yet they do not burn it; they do not even put it down. The Catholic Church strictly and wisely prohibits the reading of any books that are written by those who have fallen from the Faith, or teach a false doctrine, or impugn the Faith, or defend errors. And that for this plain and sound reason : the Church knows very well that it is not one in a thousand who is able to unravel the subtlety of infidel objections. How many of you have gone through for yourselves the evidence upon which the authen-

ticity, genuineness, and inspiration of the Book
of Daniel rests? Have you verified the canon of
the Old and New Testament? or have you mas-
tered the philosophical refutation of Atheism?
Would you advise your children to read sceptical
criticisms of Holy Scripture, or the arguments of
Deists? If not, why read them yourselves? You
know perfectly well that the human mind is capable of creating many difficulties of which it is
incapable of finding a solution. The most crude
and ignorant mind is capable of taking in what
can be said against truth. Destruction is easy;
construction needs time, industry, and care. To
gather evidence, or to ascertain the traditions
of the Church, needs learning and labour, of
which only they are capable whose life is given
to it.

This indiscriminate and fearless reading is intellectual license; but if the intellect be not mor-
tified, where will be the mortification of the will?
Look at society, as it is called. What signs are
there of mortification of the will amongst us?
When do men willingly forego anything which is
for their interest or their pleasure? When do
they leave anything undone simply for conscience,

or do anything contrary to their interest for the
sake of Jesus Christ? I am afraid that it is the
individual and the unit that does these things.
But is this religion without the Cross the religion
of Jesus Christ? Let us put it to the test. Take
the Holy Scriptures in your hands, read them as
they stand, do not explain them away: they are the
word of God. Do not say it only means this, or it
only means that. It means what it says—what God
has written—and nothing else. Now hear what
is written: 'How hardly shall they that have riches
enter into the kingdom of God! It is easier for a
camel to pass through the eye of a needle, than for
a rich man to enter into the kingdom of God.'[14]
Again, our Lord has said: 'Woe to you that are
rich; for you have received your consolation.'[15]
Again, He said: 'Enter ye in at the narrow gate;
for wide is the gate, and broad is the way that
leadeth to destruction, and many they are who go
in thereat. How narrow is the gate, and strait
is the way that leadeth to life; and few there are
that find it.'[16] And once more, when a man asked
Him: Are they few that are saved? He said: 'Strive
to enter in by the narrow gate; for many, I say to

[14] St. Mark x. 23, 25. [15] St. Luke vi. 24. [16] St. Matt. vii. 13, 14.

you, shall seek to enter, and shall not be able. But when the master of the house shall be gone in, and shall shut to the door, you shall begin to stand without, and knock at the door, saying, Lord, open to us: and he answering shall say to you, I know you not, whence you are.'[17] Once more, He says: ' Whosoever doth not carry his cross and come after Me, cannot be My disciple.'[18]

These are the warnings of our Lord and Saviour. Take the crucifix in your hand, and ask yourselves whether this is the religion of the soft, easy, worldly, luxurious days in which we live; whether the crucifix does not teach you a lesson of mortification, of self-denial, of crucifixion of the flesh, with its affections and lusts, as the Apostle says; or as our Divine Lord Himself has said: ' If thy right hand offend thee, cut it off and cast it from thee. If thy right eye offend thee, pluck it out and cast it from thee; for it is better to enter into life having one eye and one hand, than having two eyes and two hands to be cast into hell-fire.' These are the words of God, of Jesus, our merciful, loving, compassionate Lord. They are not the words of severe and heartless men. They are the words

---

[17] St. Luke xiii. 24, 25.   [18] Ib. xiv. 27.

of Divine pity, warning us that 'the wisdom of the flesh is death,' because the wisdom of the flesh is an enemy against God, and cannot be subject to the law of God.

Let us, then, be on our guard against these things, which, in their subtlety and strength, have power over us all. If we had one foot in heaven, and were to leave off mortifying ourselves, we should fall from grace.

LECTURE III.

THE REVOLT OF SOCIETY FROM GOD.

'The nation and the kingdom that will not serve Thee shall perish.' Isaias lx. 12.

THESE words are the promise of God to His Incarnate Son, the King of kings, and Lord of all the earth, which He has redeemed with His precious blood. It was to Him also that the words were spoken: 'Sit Thou at My right hand, until I make Thy enemies Thy footstool.'[1] The Son of God declares of Himself: 'I am appointed King by Him over Sion His holy mountain.'[2] Before He ascended into heaven, our Lord said to His disciples, 'All power in heaven and on earth is given unto Me;' and He promised them, saying, 'I dispose'— that is, I give—'unto you a kingdom, as My Father has disposed unto Me.'[3] This kingdom, then, is

[1] Ps. cix. 1, 2.   [2] Ibid. ii. 6.
[3] St. Matt. xxviii. 18; St. Luke xxii. 29.

the kingdom of Jesus Christ; and the prophecy here is, that any nation or any kingdom that will not serve Him shall perish. Any nation or kingdom that says, 'We will not have this Man to reign over us,' refuses the sovereignty of Jesus Christ, and thereby shall fall.

It was on the day of Pentecost that the proclamation of the coming of this kingdom was first made in a multitude of tongues, and from Jerusalem was spread throughout the world. God the Holy Ghost on that day came as the 'sound of a mighty wind,' and by tongues of fire, speaking to the eye and to the ear, in witness of His Royal presence, Majesty, and power.

I have already spoken of the revolt of the intellect from truth, and also of the revolt of the will from God. Our present subject is the revolt of man from the authority of God. When I say the revolt of man, I do not only mean of individuals, one by one, but of mankind in its organised and corporate state. It is therefore of the revolt of society from the authority of God that I am about to speak.

I have said before, that the history of the Christian society of the world may be divided into

three periods : the first, when the Church as a
spiritual society stood alone, separate from the
world, and made up of individuals gathered from
all nations, cities, and households, as a spiritual
society without contact with the civil or political society of mankind; the second, when the
Church and the civil society of the world, being
in harmony and union, after the Empire had
become Christian, were associated together in
the government and sanctification of the world;
the third is the period which for the last three hundred years has set in, of divorce, departure, and
separation, between the spiritual society of the
Church and the civil or political society of nations.
Or in other words, the first period since the coming of our Lord may be called the period of the
world under false gods, for the world was heathen;
the second was the period of the world under the
one true God; and this last period, on which we
have now entered, I am afraid must be truly and
justly named the world without God, the world
departing from the true God.

The other day a book fell into my hands, describing the progress of the world in these three
divisions. The writer says that there are three

chief cities which have affected the destinies of the
civilised world. The first is Jerusalem, from
which the Law, the religion of Israel, flowed by tradition into the world. The second is the city of
Rome, which, as the writer said—he was certainly
not a Catholic, and I believe not a Christian, and
if he were not of the house of Israel, I believe he
must have been a sceptic—was the source of the
Christian and Catholic religion, and of the society
which belongs to the Middle Ages. The third city
is the city of Paris, the new Jerusalem, the leader
of civilisation, the city of progress, and the city of
the future. While I recite these words, your own
thoughts are beginning to make their application.

At the outset of these subjects I said that
the Syllabus, published by the Sovereign Pontiff
some six or eight years ago, seems to have
turned the world upside down. It has created
commotion among peoples and kingdoms, governments and legislatures, newspapers and politicians, of whom perhaps not one in a hundred
has seen even the outside of the Syllabus, and
certainly not one in ten would take time to understand its meaning. This Syllabus is supposed to be a violent and mediæval aggression

upon the civil order of the world. Let me tell
you simply what the Syllabus is. The Gospel of
Jesus Christ—that is, Christianity—reveals a multitude of truths, and lays down a multitude of
laws. Now, the world has been perpetually
denying these truths, and violating these laws,
both intellectually and in act. The Syllabus
is a collection of eighty condemnations. Eighty
of the chief intellectual and moral errors which
have sprung up in the modern world, contrary
to the faith and morals of Christianity, have
been condemned, as they arose, by the Head of the
Church in express and explicit terms. The Syllabus is a summary of those condemnations. For
example, I will recite to you five of the errors
that are therein condemned.

They are as follows: first of all, that the
civil society of man—that is, the political order
of civil society—is the fountain and origin of all
right, and that it can be circumscribed by no authority; secondly, that in conflicts between the
spiritual and civil authorities, the civil authority is supreme, and must determine; thirdly,
that education belongs to the State, as being what
is called matter of civil competence, and ought

to be strictly secular; fourthly, that kings and princes are exempt from ecclesiastical jurisdiction; lastly, that the State ought to be separated from the Church, and the Church from the State.[4] Now, these are five of the errors which are condemned in the Syllabus; and you will easily understand that the remaining seventy-five propositions of the Syllabus are errors similar in kind. What I purpose to do is, incidentally, and without again reciting them, to show that these are five false-hoods, and are justly condemned.

There is a common axiom that passes from mouth to mouth in these days, that religion and politics have nothing to do with each other—that the Church has nothing to do with politics; that the Church must submit to the civil authorities as supreme; that politics may go their own way by themselves, and that priests and bishops, if they touch politics, go beyond their limits and exceed their powers. We hear a great deal of this talk.

Now, in the name of not only Christianity, but of common sense, I would ask you to consider for one moment the following questions: Is not the law of morals the same for a thousand men

4 Syllabus Pii IX., Propp. 39, 42, 45, 54, 55.

as for one? Is not the law of morals the same
for a nation as for an individual? Are men bound
by the moral law one by one, and are nations
and kingdoms not bound by the moral law? Is
it to be supposed that individuals, one by one, are
under obligation to keep the law of God, and that
states and kingdoms are not so bound? Are peasants bound to keep the law of the Gospel and of
the Church, and are princes and kings not bound
to keep that law? Are individuals who happen to
be poor and unlearned under the obligation to
obey Christian morality, and are not legislatures
and executive governments equally obliged? Nay,
I will say more; are they not more strictly bound
and under heavier responsibility to conform themselves to the moral law? Well, then, whence comes
the moral law? From reason and from Christianity;
from the light of reason elevated and perfected by
the Christian revelation. And to whose custody
was the Christian revelation committed? To the
Apostles and their successors, to whom our Lord
said: 'Go ye, and make disciples of all nations:
teaching them to observe whatsoever I have commanded you.' Who, then, are the guardians of
the moral law? The Apostles and their successors.

And who are their successors? The pastors of
the Church of God. And the things which He
commanded include His moral precepts as well
as the doctrines of Faith; and they bind individuals, and peoples, and nations, and kingdoms, and those who rule over them. To
talk about the separation between religion and
politics is to talk at random in those who know
no better; it is to talk impiety, or it is to talk
apostasy, in those who have understanding; for
what are politics but the morals of society, the
morals of men collected and living together under
public law? The same law which governs the
individual governs households, and the law that
governs households governs the State. The
legislature is as much bound to observe the moral
law of the Gospel as the individual, as any private
man; and therefore politics, so far from being separate, are a part of morals. They are morals
applied to the public society of men, to the public
action of nations, to the legislation of governments,
to the executive authority of princes; for which
reason, to attempt to separate between religion
and politics, to shut up the priest, as it is said, in
the sacristy, is a revolt of the world endeavouring

to shake off the yoke of Jesus Christ. If He be
the King of the world, which He has redeemed
with His precious blood, He will judge the kings
and the princes and the legislatures and the nations of this world for the laws which they have
made. And this is our present subject.

1. First of all, then, what is human society, or the
political society of the world; and who created it?
We read in histories, that such a one was the
founder of this kingdom, and such another was
the founder of that empire; but they did not
create the society. The civil order, or political society of man, is the creation of God. The
God of nature, in the day in which He created
man, created him with an innate necessity of living a social life. Society sprang from our first
parents. As soon as the family arose, the outlines
of the political order were traced upon the earth.
In the multiplication of men and of families,
sprang up the civil and political order of the
world; and that civil and political order, whatsoever form it may take, and howsoever it may be
modified, has in it three immutable principles.
It has the principle of authority, which rules; it
has the principle of obedience, which subjects

those who are under authority to its government;
it has the principle of equal and reciprocal justice
between those who are united under the same
authority. These three principles are the principles of the family, and of the household, and of
the whole civil and political order of the world.
They may be variously clothed; they may be embodied in different forms of law, according to ages
and nations; but essentially all governments and
constitutions resolve themselves at last into these
three simple laws. It is of this that the Holy
Ghost, speaking by the Apostle, says: 'Let every
soul be subject to higher powers; for there is no
power but from God; and those that are, are ordained of God. He that resisteth the power, resisteth the ordinance of God; and they that resist,
purchase to themselves damnation. For princes
are not a terror to the good work, but to the evil.
Wilt thou then not be afraid of the power? Do
that which is good. If thou do that which is evil,
fear; for he beareth not the sword in vain. For
he is God's minister: an avenger to execute
wrath upon him that doth evil.'[5]   From what
other   source   could   the   authority   to   inflict

---

[5] Rom. xiii. 1.

capital punishment be derived, save only from Him who is the Author and Giver of life? Society recognises the Divine foundation of its authority every time that justice condemns a man to die. This authority is not of human creation; it is of Divine creation. It comes from God; and civil society is therefore in itself of Divine foundation. In the order of nature, it has God for its Author. Sovereignty, then, was immediately committed by God to the society of mankind, in the act of creating it. The particular form of government, whether it be by one or by many, whether it be empire or kingdom or republic—these mutable and incidental forms of government may be determined by man; but the authority which they embody, and by which alone they exist, is always from God. Now, such is civil society. Bear in mind the principles we have laid down; because upon them all depends; all public morality and all public law, the duty of loyalty and of civil obedience, the power of capital punishment, and the mutual justice between man and man. To call in question the Divine foundation of authority, and to talk only of the rights of men, is to violate the first laws of human society. We are in the

century of revolutions, inaugurated by the gospel
of the rights of man and of the sovereignty of the
people, preached by the false prophets of this
world to deceive the nations. Men have come to
believe that the freak and caprice of the public
will is sovereign, and may at any time revoke the
authority which God has providentially ordained
in the powers that are. The word of God declares
that authority is from God, and that they who resist
the authority purchase to themselves damnation.
Now, that supreme civil authority, being of God's
own creating, is sacred, and was not left in the
world to reel and to stagger in the darkness and
instability of human ignorance and human license.
When God became incarnate, He founded His own
kingdom in the world; He instituted an authority
in which are incorporated the rights of God; He
promulgated a law which governs the conscience
of all mankind.

2. The kingdom of Jesus Christ is His Church
one and universal, and by it He exercises His
sovereignty over the nations. The commission
of His Apostles was to found a universal kingdom,
which should never be destroyed; of which the
prophet has said, ' It shall not be delivered up to

another people.'⁶ Empires have passed from people
to people, kingdoms have vanished from off the
face of the earth; but the kingdom of Jesus Christ
can never pass to any hand from that which
was pierced on Calvary. His kingdom shall en-
dure to all eternity. The Church of God on
earth is a true kingdom, reigning by its own
right. It has a right to its own existence, to its
own possessions, to its own legislature, to its
own executive, and to its own tribunals. It receives these prerogatives neither from king, nor
prince, nor people; and no human authority can
circumscribe its limits. Nay, it circumscribes the
limits of all other authority, and is itself subject
to none but God only. When the Church came
into this world, it suffered its ten persecutions.
The world, if it had been possible, would have
stifled it in its own blood; but an indefectible
life cannot perish. For three hundred years it
spread, and penetrated and pervaded the whole
civil society of the world: it entered into households, and peoples, and nations, and cities, and
kingdoms. It reached, at last, to the palace of
the Cæsars; it took possession of the imperial

⁶ Daniel ii. 44.

family; it converted the emperor on his throne:
and when it had pervaded the senate, and the
tribunals, and the whole civil life of Rome, the
empire was elevated above itself. It became regenerate by grace, and lived by a new life, and
was guided by new laws, and confirmed by new
authorities; and the civil society of the world was
born again. That which God had created in the
natural state was elevated, by its union with the
Church, to the supernatural order; the members
of it were regenerated by water and the Holy
Ghost, and became members of the kingdom of
God, illuminated by faith under the guidance of
the pastors of the Universal Church and the Vicar
of Jesus Christ. Then came to pass a change
so terrible, that the world does not contain in
history anything more fearful. Rome, which had
governed the world by its laws, and its warfare,
and its civilisation, was purged by fire and by blood.
The kingdom of Jesus Christ then took possession of the civil society of the world. Then
passed away the old civilisation, which was corrupt to the very marrow; so corrupt, that nothing
could have changed it but the baptism of fire, by
which it was cleansed. The most terrible judg-

ments of God fell upon Rome, upon the city, and upon the provinces of the Roman Empire. They were purged by wars, massacres, and pestilence; the old world was burned down to the roots, that the new civilisation and the new Christian world might spring from the earth purified by fire.

And nothing could be more beautiful, nothing more like to the vision of the Heavenly City, than the rise of this Christian civilisation. When, in the love of God, slavery began to melt away; when fathers with horror cast from them the power of life and death over their children and their slaves as a thing too hideous for Christian men; when husbands renounced with thanksgiving to their Redeemer the power of life and death over wives; when the horrors, and injustice, and abominations of the pagan domestic life gave place to the charities of Christian homes, then the whole world was lifted to a higher sphere. It had come under the light and jurisdiction of the sovereignty of Jesus Christ. Such was the growth of the world; beginning, I will say, from the time of St. Gregory the Great, the apostle of our Christianity, who reigned with a patriarchal sway over the three-and-twenty patrimonies of the Church—over Italy and the north of Africa, and the coasts of the Adriatic, and the south of France, and Sicily, and the islands of the Mediterranean. This new Christian world was the germ of modern Europe. The Pontiffs laid the foundations of a world which is now passing away—a Christian commonwealth of nations, about which men vaunt themselves as if they were its saviours, though they never cease to destroy it.

3. And then came another epoch, when, in the solemnities of Christmas-day of the year 800, St. Leo III. crowned Charlemagne at the tomb of the Apostle, and made him the Emperor of the West. That act, done in the midst of tribulation and danger, when the times were dark with all manner of evil, was the beginning of a new era. There sprang up in the world for some seven hundred years a Christendom in which the kings and princes of Europe acknowledged the sovereignty of Jesus Christ: the nations and the kingdoms served Him, and inherited the benediction promised to those that acknowledge His supreme rights. In order that we may better understand what, in those ages of faith, was the belief of men as to the civil power, let us look

at the ceremony of the consecration of a king.
Nowadays we hear of coronations, but we hear
no more of the consecration of kings. But a
coronation, even in the tradition of England, takes
place in the old Abbey of Westminster, and with
certain rites which remain, mutilated indeed, but
taken chiefly from the ancient Catholic ritual. I
will shortly describe what the ancient ritual
was. The prince who was to be consecrated, for
three days before, fasted as a preparation. On the
day of his consecration he came to the sanctuary
of the church, where the metropolitan and his
suffragans received him. He then, first upon his
knees before the altar made solemn oath to Almighty God, to observe and cause to be observed,
according to his knowledge and his power, for
the sake of the Church and of his people, law, justice, and peace, according to the laws of the land
and the canons of the Church. He then lay pros-
trate before the altar, like a bishop when he is
consecrated; the litanies were chanted, the same
litanies which are sung in our solemn ordinations.
Then, kneeling before the altar, he received the
unction. He was anointed in the right arm,
which is the arm of strength, and on the shoulder,

typical of royal power; as in the prophecy, 'The government is upon His shoulder.'[7] He then received the sword, with this admonition, 'Remember that the saints conquered kingdoms, not by the sword, but by faith.' After this, the crown was put upon his head, with the prayer that he might wear it in mercy and in justice; and the sceptre was then placed in his hands, in token of the authority of law. After that, the Holy Mass was celebrated; and in that Mass he received the Holy Communion of the precious body and blood of Jesus Christ, from the hands of the consecrating bishop. These solemn acts in themselves portrayed what were the relations of Christian law and fidelity between the chief rulers of nations and of kingdoms, and the sovereignty of Jesus Christ.

4. Such was once the Christian world. What is it now? Look at Christian Europe. Read history for the last three hundred years. Briefly, for briefly it must be, I will touch upon its main points. Three hundred years ago, Germany and the greater part of northern Europe—Sweden, Norway, Denmark, England, Scotland, to say nothing of other smaller countries—separated

7 Isaias ix. 6.

themselves formally from the unity of the Faith and Church, and therein of the supreme authority of the Vicar of Jesus Christ. What straightway followed? The civil power, which until that time had been obedient to the laws of faith and of Christian morality, thenceforward went its way alone, choosing and determining for itself. The most terrible persecutions, to prison and to death, for the sake of religion, sprang up in every country; and the two authorities, civil and spiritual, which God has made distinct and has committed to separate hands, were united in the person of princes. The civil supremacy and the ecclesiastical supremacy were claimed for the crown, and civil rulers invested themselves with prerogatives which can be borne by the Vicar of Jesus Christ alone. The authority over conscience, religion, and the worship of God belongs only to those to whom He has committed it. Wheresoever the conscience and the soul enter in, man is free from all authority of men. No king, nor prince, nor legislature, has power to make law or ordinance over my conscience. He may take my life, but my faith he cannot touch. It was a violation of the Divine law: and bitterly

and in blood the people that were torn from the
unity of the Church suffered for that deed. I will
say nothing of Ireland—the memories of Ireland
are too mournful, too profoundly dark—but England, which then was united, which then had one
faith and one worship, has been miserably rent,
cut asunder in religion, until one half of the
English people no longer belong to the religion which was set up by law three hundred years
ago. And those who have separated from it are
divided and subdivided again into innumerable
religious fractions; and in that one body, which is
held together by the law, what a dying out of
faith, what denials of Christianity, what oppositions
of teachers against each other, what separations,
what bondage of conscience, what violations of
Christian liberty! From what source are all these
evils? From the usurpation of the civil authority,
which assumed to itself to be the head and supreme judge in religion.

But I pass this by. These were only the beginning of troubles which fell upon the nations
separated from the unity of the Church. There
was also a flood of evils in countries that still
continued to be of that unity. In France, in Aus-

tria, in parts of Italy, in Spain, in Portugal, princes who still professed to be Catholic, assumed authority to meddle with religion, with worship, with education, though not with faith. They did indeed profess that they could not touch faith; but discipline and all things outside of faith they claimed as subject to their jurisdiction.

I have said that there is, in all countries, a disposition to depart from the unity of the Christian civilisation which the providence of God has ordained. The conflicts which began three hundred years ago have been everywhere accomplishing themselves. In Austria some twenty years ago, in Italy the other day, it was declared that the Church and the State were no longer united; that is to say, that the sovereignty of Jesus Christ was no longer acknowledged by the civil power, and that the political order of the world was claimed by man for himself. The 'kingdoms and the nations' would no longer serve the sovereignty of Jesus Christ. The other day, two laws were passed in Italy, the one to forbid the teaching of Christian doctrine (that is, the Catechism) in the schools of the poor, the other to forbid the teaching of theology in the universities of the kingdom.

5. Thus far, I have touched upon the creation of the civil power; secondly, upon its consecration by Christianity; thirdly, upon the harmony and union between the civil and the spiritual powers when united; fourthly, on the separation and divorce which has been accomplishing itself between them. I now come to the last point, which is a consequence of that divorce—the desecration of civil society, the stripping-off, the effacing of the sacred and Christian character from all political institutions.

For clearness, I will give an example of what I mean; and I do it sadly, and with the greatest tenderness of sympathy. If any word I speak should seem to be wounding to noble, Christian, Catholic, chivalrous France, I disclaim beforehand whatever may seem to come from my lips. In the year 1789, as I told you the other night, was published to the world a document called the *Principles of the Rights of Man*. I told you then, that in that document we find nothing about the duties of man, or the rights of God. The rights of man, indeed, are there; as if man were the lord and king of all things: as if he had no duties to anybody, and no one had rights over him. What was the consequence of this beginning? There

were two of the greatest pestilences at that time
spreading in France, the forerunners and causes of
its downfall—the infidel philosophy of Voltaire,
and the flagrant immorality of Rousseau; the two
false prophets, who destroyed the one the faith,
the other the morals of society. You will remember how the worship of Christianity was then
abolished, the name of Jesus Christ blasphemed,
the church of Notre Dame profaned; Reason, per-
sonified as my tongue refuses to describe, set upon
the altar. Atheism took possession of men's minds,
or rather of their lives. And there came a day
when, as by a concession towards belief, the As-
sembly voted the existence of the Supreme Being.
You know what followed: a reign of terror, blood,
blasphemy; horrors beyond the imagination of
man; revolutions in every city; civil war in the
streets; an infidel empire. At last, Christianity
was restored as a public policy; and no doubt,
under that politic device, faithful men and faithful
pastors began once more to do their work. Souls
once more were saved; but the heart of faith was
sick unto death.

Such was France for a long period of years;
and the seeds of infidelity were cast far and wide.

They sank so deep, that never to this day has Atheism been finally eradicated. In the midst of that noble, Christian, Catholic people, the roots of infidelity are now so deeply set, and the taint of indifferentism is so wide, that all the prayers, labours, sufferings of the faithful and fervent cannot restore to France its Christian laws, and the sovereignty of Jesus Christ. After awhile, came a restoration; you know with what results. I will not go into detail. We have seen, I think, some five revolutions, and in three of them blood running in the streets. But all this has passed away; and the horrors of the past are pale in the horrors before us at this moment. We used to look back upon the first French revolution as a time of such exquisite terror, that I, for my part, have often wondered how our forefathers could have endured the daily tidings of misery and blood so near to their doors; but you and I have been hearing worse, day by day, for weeks, and in this last week worse than all. The other day we read these words: ' In a little while all religion will disappear from the schools of the Commune; the crucifix will disappear as a violation of liberty of conscience.' A little while afterwards there was a question whether or not the churches should be closed; and it was answered, ' That the churches be kept open, and that in them Atheism shall be taught, to disabuse the minds of men from the prejudice of belief.' And do we, then, wonder that the chief pastor of that flock and some score of his faithful clergy are cast into prison ? and in this moment of horrible suspense God only knows whether they be among the living or the dead.

It is almost out of place to quote the words I now repeat ; but they are so intensely horrible, that lest I should seem to exaggerate, I here transcribe them. They are from Comte, one of the false prophets who has been contributing to the ruin of France by the moral and intellectual action of his false philosophy for the last thirty years. He is held in honour by some in England, and has disciples among us, who teach the same intellectual enormities. These are his words : ' In the name of the past and the future, the servants of humanity, both its philosophical and practical servants —come forward to claim as their due the general direction of this world. Their object is to constitute at length a real Providence in all departments, moral, intellectual, and material.

Consequently, they exclude once for all, from political supremacy, all the different servants of God, Catholic, Protestant, or Deist, as being at once behindhand and a cause of disturbance.'[8] I told you in the beginning, of the three cities typical of civilisation, and that the new Jerusalem of progress is Paris. We see that new Jerusalem at this moment illuminated, not with the light of God and of the Lamb, but by the flames of its burning palaces, and by the conflagration of its homes. And to what one supreme cause is this to be ascribed? To the rejection of God and of His Christ, to the rejection of the sovereignty of our Divine Redeemer. 'The nation and the kingdom that will not serve Him shall perish;' and noble, Christian, Catholic France, except it acknowledge once more the sovereignty of Jesus Christ, by that Divine law of prophecy must perish. But I have better hopes. I know, from my own personal knowledge, that through the provinces of that noble people there are millions who are true and faithful. They are casting off, by the almighty help of God, the tyranny and the dominion of a corrupt and infidel sect.

---

[8] Catechism of Positive Religion, preface.

It is more than time to make an end: I will therefore draw a general conclusion from what I have said, that the unimaginable horrors, of which Paris is at this moment the field, come from the revolt of civil society from God. They are the offspring, the legitimate, the lineal working out, of the principles of infidelity and impiety which were set in motion a century ago. And let statesmen and politicians lay to heart, that the first rising, in 1789, was a rising against the king and those that surrounded him; the next rising, in 1830 and 1848, was of the middle class against those that were immediately above them; but the rising now is the rising of the masses, of the multitudes, who, having been neglected, outcast, and therefore morally outlawed, have been robbed of their Christian education. They have grown up a terrible generation, to be the scourge and the overthrow of civil society. I need not, then, repeat that Pius IX., in the Syllabus, taught wisely and well, that it is a falsehood, and an error to be condemned by Christian men, to say that the civil society of the world is the fountain and origin of all right, and cannot be circumscribed. The Church of God and God Himself are the fountain

and the origin of rights higher than the civil
state; and the authority of God and of His laws
circumscribes the authority of the civil order.
Next, it is a falsehood, and an error justly condemned, to say that, when the spiritual and the
civil authorities are in conflict, the contention shall
be determined by the superior authority of the
civil power. The spiritual authority of God and
of the Christian laws must circumscribe and limit
the claims of the civil authority. Thirdly, it is a
falsehood and an error to say that education is a
matter of civil competence and ought to be secular.
The education of Christian men must be Christian.
The education of baptised children must be according to the faith of their baptism. Nothing
can educate the heart, the soul, and the conscience
but the laws of God. Again, it is a falsehood and
an error to say that kings and princes are exempt
from the superior jurisdiction of God and of His
Church. They are bound like others, and bound
with a heavier responsibility than others, and will
have to give a heavier reckoning before the tribunal
of the King of kings. And lastly, to say that the
Church ought to be separated from the State, and
the State from the Church, is a falsehood and an

error to be condemned; because, in the natural
order, the State is God's creation, and, in the
supernatural order, the Church is God's creation,
and these two ought to be in harmony and in
union. They ought to act in concord, co-operat-
ing with one another to the highest ends of man.

And now there are two plain truths which I will
add by way of corollaries from all that I have said.
The civil powers of the world, in separating themselves from the authority of God and of His Church,
are committing suicide; it is political self-murder.
They are condemning themselves to one of two
inevitable results — either to the despotism of
military dictators, or to the worst form of tyranny,
the tyranny of revolutions. The civil powers of
the world at this moment are standing between
two great movements, and between them they
must make their choice. There is, on the one
hand, the One Holy Catholic Church, with its
Divine authority, its Divine faith, its Divine laws,
and its Divine obligations, spreading throughout
the world, penetrating into all nations. This there
is on one side—and this is in the noonday light.
But there is on the other a society which is in
the darkness of midnight: the deadly antagonist

of the Church. It is one, because it is compactly united: it is unholy, for it springs from Satan: it is universal, for it is international; it is invisible, because it is hid out of the sight of men; and that is the universal international revolution of secret societies, allied together for the common purpose of overturning, if it were possible (as it is not), the Church of God, and of overturning (as it is easily possible) all civil governments on earth. Between these two alternatives, the civil rulers of to-day have to make their choice. ' O ye kings, understand : receive instruction, you that judge the earth.'[9]   The choice is before you; civil life or death : choose promptly, that you may live.

But, I fear, the choice is already made. If there be one thing that has been derided, scoffed at, cast out, misrepresented, in these last twenty years, it is the Temporal Power of the Pope. Yet what is it but the recognition of the sovereignty of Jesus Christ over men and over races, over public law, over the whole of Christendom—the recognition that there is a King in heaven, Who is represented upon earth, and that on earth there is one from whom the interpretation of His law, and the

[9] Ps. ii. 10.

sentence of His truth, comes with supreme authority? In this person alone are united together the two authorities, civil and spiritual; in
order that, in all other nations of the world, those
two authorities shall be separate: so that tyranny
over the consciences of men and violation of the
freedom of religious conviction shall be rendered
impossible, because kings and princes and rulers
are limited by a superior authority in all things
that are spiritual. And inasmuch as that supreme
spiritual authority has been, by Divine Providence,
in a visible and marvellous manner, freed from all
subjection to emperors or kings, having a perfect
independence of his own, owing only to his Divine
Master in heaven the account that he must give
—that Providence of God is being visibly justified
at this moment by the revolutions, now assailing
all countries which have cast off their allegiance to
the Christian Church. I see no hope for the Christian civilisation of the world, unless men turn back
again to the true foundation of Christian society,
and acknowledge that this dark and bitter period
of revolution has sprung from a rising against the
authority of the Church of God, and that revolt
and unbelief are the curse and scourge of Europe.

In the beginning I said that this subject, though it seems to be of a public and political kind, is also intrinsically moral and religious. It comes home to our consciences. To-morrow, it may be, in the first newspaper that falls in your way, you will hear the principles of which I have been speaking denied and denounced. It is necessary, therefore, that we should, from time to time, turn back again to these great laws and principles of faith. They sprang from faith, and they belong to the morality of faith.

I have said these things because I am convinced that it is necessary you should be on your guard. Do not be deceived by the silvery sounds of 'liberty,' of 'freedom,' of 'public rights,' of 'the rights of man,' and of those rights which I spoke of last time, and for very shame will not utter again. Be on your guard. Do not be seduced or carried away by the talk and clamour of a revolting and unbelieving age. Remember the words of the Son of God: 'You shall know the truth, and the truth shall make you free.'[10] 'If the Son shall make you free, you shall be free indeed.'[11]

Liberty without Jesus Christ is the worst of

[10] St. John viii. 32.   [11] Ibid. 36.

bondage. The service of Jesus Christ is true liberty. Remember His own words : 'Come to Me, all you that labour, and are burdened, and I will refresh you. Take up My yoke upon you, and learn of Me ; because I am meek, and humble of heart, and you shall find rest for your souls. For My yoke is sweet, and My burden light.'[12] This alone is the way of liberty. Liberty is in the heart. True liberty is in the service of Him who must 'reign until He hath put all His enemies under His feet.'[13]

[12] St. Matt. xi. 28-30.   [13] 1 Cor. xv. 25.

LECTURE IV.

' If the world hate you, know ye that it hath hated Me before you. If you had been of the world, the world would love its own; but because you are not of the world, but I have chosen you out of the world, therefore the world hateth you.' St. John xv. 18, 19.

MASK it as we may, there is an irreconcilable enmity between God and the world. The Christian world may put on the vestments and bear the name of Christianity, but it is the world, after all. Not that there is enmity on God's part against the world; for ' God so loved the world as to give His only-begotten Son; that whosoever believeth in Him, may not perish, but may have life everlasting.'[1] But ' the friendship of this world

---

[1] St. John iii. 16.

is an enemy against God,' as we have already seen, because it is not subject to the law of God, nor can be.

This then is the meaning of our Lord's words when He said to the Apostles, who were becoming daily conscious of the hatred of men against them: 'If the world hate you, know ye that it hath hated Me before you.'[2] If you had been of the world — servants, friends, flatterers of the world—the world would have loved its own, it would have recognised its own reflection, its own mind, its own livery; but because you are not of the world, but I, by grace and special election, have chosen you out of the world, therefore, for that very reason, because you have My mark, because you bear My name, because, in some degree, you share My likeness; therefore the world hateth you. This enmity is perpetual: it exists at this day, it will exist to the end. Between God and the world there may be an apparent truce; there never can be peace. God is immutable; His perfections cannot change. The world is malicious, and from its malice it will not change; and therefore, as the Apostle says, 'What participation

[2] St. John xv. 18.

hath justice with injustice? what concord hath Christ with Belial?[3] God, then, when manifest in the flesh, in the person of the eternal Son, was the object of the world's chief hatred; and the world, after wreaking upon Him all that scorn, derision, insults could effect, nailed Him upon the cross. The shame and the passion of the Incarnate Son of God has been the inheritance of His Church. For what is the Church of Christ but the body of Christ? Or, in other words, it is Christ mystical, the mystical person made up, as St. Augustine says, of the divine Head in heaven and of the body spread throughout the world; 'one man, one collective person.' The enmity and the hatred which the world bore to Him has descended from generation to generation, as the heirloom of His body. This, then, is Christ. Now what is Antichrist?

In the beginning I disclaimed all intention of entering into the exposition of unfulfilled prophecies. I am speaking of patent facts under our eyes. They are sufficient, because they give us principles and warnings to govern our conduct. Nevertheless, I must say, in passing, that if there

---

[3] 2 Cor. vi. 14, 15.

be anything evident in the plain words of Holy
Scripture, if there be anything explicitly declared
by the Christian Fathers, and anything distinctly
taught by the theologians of the Church, it is this ;
that Antichrist, though taken to express a dif-
fused spirit which pervades systems and incorporates itself in various forms in all ages, nevertheless will be, towards the latter days, impersonated
in one who shall be the head and the chief of that
Antichristian spirit and system, and shall use all
his power against the Name and the Church of
Jesus Christ. This I now set aside, as being beyond my purpose. I am speaking of the Antichristian spirit which manifests itself either in
individuals or in whole systems, sometimes in
whole nations. Just as the electricity which is
suspended in the air is breathed unconsciously, so
the Antichristian spirit exists in what is called
the Christian world in its present fragmentary and
divided state. And this is the subject with which
to-night I must conclude that which I have endeavoured, but very imperfectly, to say.

I have already drawn out before you the dis-
tinction between the world as it was before it had
faith in Christ, and as it became when the Christian

Faith was received by the nations which were fe-
derated in what we call Christendom; and lastly,
as it is now, since the world, having once been
Christian, has for the last three hundred years
been ceasing to be so.

Now, the Apostle has given us three marks of
this final and Antichristian apostasy from the Faith.
The first mark is given by St. John, where he says
that 'they went out from us, but they were not of
us; for if they had been of us, they would no doubt
have remained with us;[4] that is to say, separation
or schism, actual and visible departure from the
unity of the Church. The second mark is a denial of
the Incarnation of the Son of God. St. John says
in his second epistle : 'Many seducers are gone out
into the world, who confess not that Jesus Christ
is come in the flesh. This is a seducer and an antichrist.'[5] The third mark is given by St. Jude: 'These
are they who separate themselves, sensual men,'
which word signifies, in the original, men of natural
intellect and natural reason; it does not necessarily mean sensual in the grosser sense, though
it leads to it. 'These are they who separate themselves, sensual, not having the Spirit,'[6] that is, they

---

[4] 1 St. John ii. 19.   [5] 2 St. John 7.   [6] St. Jude 19.

reject the Holy Ghost, and the work of the Spirit of God in the world. This third mark is the rejection of the revelation of the day of Pentecost, with all those truths, laws, and authorities, which took their rise from the coming of the Spirit of Truth. These then are the three marks of the world departing from Christianity.

If you look back over the last three hundred years, you will see that whole nations have departed from the visible unity of the Church. They have come to deny that any visible unity was ever instituted; they deny their separation by denying the law. 'Where there is no law, there is no transgression,'[7] the Apostle says; and it is necessary to deny the law of unity in order to justify the separation. Springing up from those bodies separated from the unity of the Church has come, first, Socinianism or Unitarianism, as it is commonly called—rejection of the mystery of the Most Holy Trinity, of the Godhead of the Incarnate Son, of the work of the Holy Spirit of God, first in His Divine authority, perpetually and infallibly guiding and speaking through the Church; next, in His operation through the Holy Sacraments; and

[7] Rom. iv. 15.

thirdly, His workings of grace in the individual soul. How extensively, both in speculation and in practice, these truths are at this time rejected by · many who retain the name of Christians, you well know. And once more, if you look at nations in which these departures from truth are to be found, you will find that the whole course of legislation for the last three hundred years has been, as I have already pointed out, a perpetual departure from the laws of Christianity. Forasmuch, then, as men are interminably and irreconcilably divided, it is impossible that the legislature can touch upon matters of Christianity or of religion without conflicting with the private convictions or the private opinions of some men or some bodies of men; and therefore the civil powers of the world in despair have taken refuge in the policy of eliminating and excluding altogether from the public laws of the land all reference to anything but those fundamental moral axioms which are to be found not only in Christianity, but, almost without exception, in the order of nature.

There is to be found in such individuals as I have been describing, in such nations and in such

governments, a worldly character, which partakes
of the Antichristian spirit. These may seem to be
harsh and severe terms, but 'he that is not with
Me, is against Me.'[8] They are the words of Jesus
Christ Himself. There is no neutrality in matters
of faith ; and the tendency of all peoples, nations,
and governments that have ceased to legislate
positively in a Christian sense, is to legislate at
last in a sense that is, first beside, then contrary
to, Christianity.

What I have now to do is to draw out the
particular points in which the Antichristian spirit
is to be found working in society, and therefore
round about us.

1. The first illustration I will give is this:
the impatience of all revealed authority, as
entering in any degree into the control of the
thoughts or the will of men, or into the action of government. There is a disposition in
public opinion, and in public men, and in the
masses, to say : 'Politics have nothing to do with
religion.' This I have answered before ; and I am
going on to show one more application of this
false maxim. It is commonly said, that what is

[8] St. Matt. xii. 30.

called 'dogma' is a limitation of the liberty of the
human reason; that it is degrading to a rational
being to allow his intellect to be limited by dog-
matic Christianity; that liberty of thought, liberty
of discovery, the progress of advancing truth,
apply equally to Christianity, if it be true, as to
all other kinds of truth; and therefore a man,
when he allows his intellect to be subjected by
dogma, has allowed himself to be brought into
an intellectual bondage. Well, now, let me test
the accuracy and the value of this supposed axiom.
The science of astronomy has been a traditional
science for I know not how many generations of
men. It has been perpetually advancing, expanding, testing, completing its discoveries, and
demonstrating the truth of its theories and its
inductions. Now, every single astronomical truth
imposes a limit upon the intellect of man. When
once the truth has been demonstrated there is no
further question about it. The intellect of man
is thenceforward limited in respect of that truth.
He cannot any longer contradict it without losing
his dignity as a man of science—I might say, as a
rational creature. It appears, therefore, that the
certainty of every scientific truth imposes a cer-

tain limitation upon the intellect; and yet scientific men tell us that, in proportion as science is expanded by new discoveries and new demonstrations, the field of knowledge is increased. Well, then, I ask, in the name of common justice and of common sense, why may I not apply this to revelation? If the possession of a scientific truth, with its complete scientific accuracy, be not a limitation, and is therefore no degradation of the human intellect, but an elevation and an expansion of its range, why should the defined and precise doctrines of revelation be a bondage against which the intellect of man ought to rebel? On the contrary, I affirm that every revealed doctrine is a limitation imposed upon the field of error. The regions in which men may err become narrower, because the boundaries of truth are pushed farther, and the field of truth is enlarged. The liberty of the human intellect is therefore greater, because it is in possession of a greater inheritance of certainty. And yet, if there be one superstition which at the present day is undermining more than any other the faith of men, it is the notion that belief in the positive dogma of Christianity is a slavish limitation of the intellectual freedom of man.

I

Once more, it is said that the revealed morality of Christianity is a limitation of the freedom
of the human will. I must ask your forbearance
for speaking of such a topic to you; for I ought to
suppose that there is no one here so darkened, I
must say, in heart as well as in understanding as
to think that Christian morality, by limiting the
actions and even the thoughts, and regulating the
freedom of the will, imposes upon them a bondage
unworthy of men. Nevertheless, there are some
who cry out against the laws of morality which are
taught by the Church of Jesus Christ, as being an
interference with human liberty. Now, what does
the morality of the Christian law forbid? First, all
things that are unjust. Surely no man will plead
for a liberty to act unjustly. Secondly, all things
that are hurtful to himself or to his neighbour. A
man will not plead for liberty to do hurt to his
neighbour. Will he plead for liberty to do hurt to
himself? to commit suicide, for instance—that is, for
the liberty of self-murder? Lastly, it forbids the
commission of those things that are mortal before
God, of acts that are deadly in their consequences.
In the name of reason I would ask you, is there any
limit imposed upon the liberty of men in taking

from them the freedom to drink poison, and laying upon them the bondage of living on food? And yet the laws of the Church impose no other limitation on any man. Nevertheless, the spirit of insubordinate intellect and insubordinate will, fostered by schism and by unbelief, is spreading fast at this day; and men are crying out against the authority of revelation as a yoke and a bondage.

And it is further said, that revelation has nothing to do with the civil authority of the world. I hope that I have already given reason enough for affirming that the civil authority of the world, if it be not founded upon revelation, is, nevertheless, so guided, confirmed, and strengthened by it, that it cannot long subsist without it. If it lose the support and guidance of revelation, it soon falls into the natural order, with all the penalties of dissolution. Now, what limit does revelation impose upon the civil power? It limits authority, in those that bear it, to the execution of justice and mercy; it forbids tyranny and despotism. It limits the freedom of subjects by the law of conscience, to obedience and submission; and it teaches man to observe the equal rights of other men and the duties which he owes to his fellows. It teaches to all men the sacred law which lies at the base of all just legislation: 'Do to others as you would have men do to you.' These are the primary laws of justice and of charity. I ask whether these are limitations hostile to the freedom or to the prosperity of states? In one word, the only conservative spirit, a phrase we hear even to weariness — that which alone upholds, confirms, and renders indissoluble the civil society of mankind—is Christianity, or the revelation and the laws of Jesus Christ. Nevertheless, if there be anything which the public opinion of most countries, separated from the unity of the Church— and, I am sorry to say, the public opinion of some countries which profess still to be within that unity—resents, it is the entrance of the laws of revelation into the sphere of their legislature. I shall not say too much by adding, that there exists a widespread animosity against the one only Church which will not accept of royal or legislative supremacy. There is in the world one Church which has never accepted of royal supremacy in faith or morals. It has never accepted Acts of Parliament or legislative enactments as superior to its own canonical legislation and to its own spiritual executive. Now, I believe, that is the only Church against which public animosity and even private hostility is levelled in any marked degree. All other bodies are treated as national, domestic, and innocuous. They are not to be feared. If they have a will of their own, they have no power to exert it. But the Church which absolutely refuses the supremacy of all civil powers is looked upon at once as aggression, invasion, and a menace to the supreme authority of public opinion, and, it may be, of princes.

2. Why is this? In one word, because the enmity which assails revelation falls upon it chiefly as incorporated in the Church. It exists there as in a definite, visible, palpable form. In the sphere of intellect men cannot lay their hands on revelation. It is, like the light of day, impalpable. In the order and the sphere of ideas it is intangible altogether; but, embodied in the Church, it becomes a visible and palpable impersonation, standing in the place of its Divine Head, on whom men laid their hands while He was within arm's length. But now, at the right hand of God, He is beyond their reach. His body, however, is here; and therefore He cried out to Saul on the way to Damascus,

'Saul, Saul, why persecutest thou Me?'—that is to say, His Church upon earth is Himself. The same spirit, therefore, which was directed against Him while He was within the reach of men is now directed against His Church, which is still palpable and within their grasp. It incorporates dogma, it enforces discipline, it wields authority, it legislates, it decrees, it inflicts censures, it sits in judgment upon the conduct of men, of private persons, of professors, of nations, of princes. Come what may, it will not be silent. Let men threaten as they will, it still speaks as the Prince of the Apostles, who said: 'If it be just in the sight of God to hear you rather than God, judge ye.'[9]

This Divine liberty of speech, which began in the lips of the Son of God Himself, passed to His Apostles, and from them has passed to His Church. It has spoken freely throughout all ages, and throughout all the world. The prerogatives of the Church are especially offensive to the world. Our Lord said to the chief of the Apostles, and through him to them all, and through them to their successors to the end of the world: 'I will give to thee the keys of the kingdom of heaven;

[9] Acts iv. 19.

and whatsoever thou shalt bind upon earth, it shall
be bound also in heaven; and whatsoever thou shalt
loose upon earth, it shall be loosed also in heaven.'[10] We do not explain away these words. We
teach them as we received them from our Divine
Master. They mean that what the authority of
His Church binds on earth, is by Him ratified in
heaven; that there is a twofold and concurrent
action, which in effect is identical, between the
authority of the Church on earth, and the authority
of its Divine Head in heaven. And therefore,
when the Apostle said: ' If any man love not our
Lord Jesus Christ, let him be anathema maran-
atha,' he pronounced a judicial sentence which had
its effect, though it was not yet seen to follow, as
when our Divine Master said to the barren fig-tree,
' May no fruit grow on thee henceforward for
ever,'[11] and the fig-tree withered away; and as
when Peter rebuked Ananias and Sapphira, his
sentence was straightway executed. We may
not see, indeed, these palpable and immediate results; but we know with Divine certainty that the
effects of excommunication will surely follow. In
the Epistle to the Corinthians the Apostle, writing

[10] St. Matt. xvi. 19.   [11] Ibid. xxi. 19.

of the incestuous man, said: 'I, indeed absent in
body, but present in spirit, have already judged,
as though I were present, him who hath so
done: in the name of our Lord Jesus Christ, you
being gathered together with my spirit, with
the power of the Lord Jesus Christ, to deliver
such a one to Satan for the destruction of the
flesh, that the spirit may be saved in the day of
our Lord Jesus Christ.'[12] These are not empty
threats; they are judicial pronouncements of a
Divine authority. Will any one tell me that this
power has ceased in the world? Read the history
of sacrilege against the Holy See; or read, if you
will, the history of sacrilege written by a well-
known writer of the Church of England two hundred years ago, who believed this Christian law,
and verified it in the history of those who, three
hundred years back, committed or partook of sacrilege in England. Search through history, and find
me an example of sacrilege which has not sooner
or later met its doom. There is a God who
judgeth the earth; and He judges it through
those laws which He incorporated in the authority
of His Church. He executes His judgments by His

[12] 1 Cor. v. 3-5.

own Divine providence, when and how He wills.
Now against that which I have said, there is a spirit
of hostility and contempt, at least assumed. I
say assumed contempt; because, under the ap-
pearance of derision, there is a sharpness in the
tone which shows the animosity of fear.

3. There is yet another kind of Antichristian
enmity, which finds its way into the hearts of many
who would be startled and wounded if they
were told that their spirit is Antichristian. If
there be a subject against which public writers,
public speakers, and public talkers are perpetually
declaiming, it is what is called the religious life—
the life of monks and of nuns. The whole literature of countries that are not Catholic is full of
all manner of tales, calumnies, slanders, fables,
fictions, absurdities, on the subject of monks and
nuns. Now, why should men trouble themselves
so much about it? Why cannot they leave peace-
ful people to use their own liberty? No man or
woman is compelled to be monk or nun; and if
by perversion of light, if by idiotcy, as the world
calls it, any should be found who desire to live
the life of monk or nun, why should public opinion
trouble itself so much about the matter? Men

may become Mormons; they may settle down at
Salt Lake; they may join any sect; they may
adopt any practices which do not bring them
under the hands of the police, and the public
opinion of this country does not trouble itself
about them. What, then, is the reason why it
troubles itself about the religious life? Because
it is a life of perfection; because it is a life which
is a rebuke to the world, a direct and diametrical
contradiction of the axioms and maxims by which
the world governs itself. The world is therefore
conscious of the rebuke, and uneasy under that
consciousness. When the Son of God came into
the world, all men turned against Him except the
few whom He called to be His disciples. Even a
heathen philosopher has recorded this belief: that
if a perfectly just man were ever to be seen on
earth, he would be out of place and a wonder;
or, as we may say, a monster amongst men. And
why? Because, in the universal injustice of mankind, he would stand alone, and his life would be
a rebuke. In Holy Scripture this is described, as
it were, with a pencil of light. In the Book of
Wisdom, the men of this world say: 'Let us lie
in wait for the just; because he is not for our turn,

and he is contrary to our doings, and upbraideth us with transgressions of the law, and divulgeth against us the sins of our way of life . . . he abstaineth from our ways as from filthiness, and he preferreth the latter end of the just . . . he calleth himself the son of God . . . he is grievous unto us even to behold.'[13] The finger of the Holy Spirit has here traced the real analysis of this animosity against the religious life. Some years ago I remember reading a paper upon 'The Extinct Virtues,' and what were they? Obedience, chastity, voluntary poverty. If so, then, the eight beatitudes are extinct. I do not suppose the world would accept this. They would count me a severe and an unjust accuser if I were to say that disorder, unchastity, and the love of riches are the ascendent virtues of modern society. But if obedience, chastity, and voluntary poverty are extinct, their opposites must be in the ascendent. Of this I am sure: that the prevalent spirit amongst men at this day is to feel a secret hostility against a life which surpasses their own; and therefore it is that we hear these tales, fables, slanders, fictions about monks and nuns; and that

[13] Wisd. ii. 12-16.

we have books like *La Religieuse* and *Le Mau-
dit;* or romances about the acts of ex-Bene-
dictine nuns at Naples, and suchlike; or that
which is the gospel of a multitude of people—
though it has been exposed a hundred times
over as a stupid self-refuting imposture, condemned and exposed by positive local proof and
distinct documentary evidence—the history of
' Maria Monk.' Nevertheless, this abomination is
printed and reprinted, and bought and sold, because there is a gross morbid taste to which it
panders, and a diseased hatred which it gratifies.
It is not only against the life of perfection, but
against every reflection of God, wheresoever it
may be seen, that this Antichristian animosity directs itself. And there are two things which,
perhaps, are more hated, more intensely and more
bitterly attacked, than any others.

The first is the confessional, because in it the
priest sits in the name of God, hearing all things
in His stead, with his lips closed, and ready to shed
his blood rather than break that seal. He holds a
power which was given him in the Apostles on that
night when our Divine Lord breathed upon them,
and said, ' Receive ye the Holy Ghost; whose sins

you shall forgive, they are forgiven them, and whose sins you shall retain, they are retained.'[14] He sits there invested with that authority, a witness to the day of judgment; and the self-accusation of men is the prelude and the preparation for the last day. The world, if it could, would pull the Last Judge off His throne; but, because He is beyond the reach of its arm, they pull the priest out of the confessional.

The other thing against which the enmity of men is directed, is the presence of Jesus in the Blessed Sacrament. The Sacrament of the Altar is the manifestation of the Divine presence; it is the incorporation of the Divine love, sanctity, and power; and against these things the Antichristian revolt hurls itself as the chief object of its hatred: as but the other day, if our tidings speak the truth, the Blessed Sacrament was sacrilegiously mocked and scattered in the midst of blaspheming men and weeping women.

4. There is yet another object of this animosity. What I said last leads on immediately to the priesthood. Englishmen have heard from childhood so much about priestcraft, and about being priest-rid-

---

[14] St. John xx. 22, 23.

den, and about bad priests, that they grow up with a
belief that a priest is a noxious creature, a sort of
fera natura, something specially venomous, anti-
social, perilous to the commonwealth of men.
What is the priesthood? The priesthood is a
body of men, instituted by our Saviour, into which
any man of you, if he has the will and the fitness,
may freely enter to-morrow. It is not a caste;
it is not Freemasonry; it is not a secret society
of moral assassins, nor a close corporation of
tyrannous men. It is open to all; it has no
secrets but the sins of those that repent. It is
the most democratic of all the governments on
earth: the sons of peasants and of ploughmen
are at this day standing at our altars and sitting
upon the throne of Apostles. The Holy Council
of Trent lays upon the conscience of bishops, in
founding their seminaries, to replenish them rather
with the children of the poorer classes. The
priesthood, therefore, is so open to every man,
that if there be a secret craft, a priestcraft, to
be learnt, let him come and learn it; he has only
to blame himself if he does not know all about us.
We have no mysteries, or ciphers, or masonic
signs. The priesthood and the theology which

makes the priest are open to everybody; it is not
like secret societies, which hide themselves from
the light and labour underground. The priesthood
is in noonday, standing at the altar, and everybody may know what it is; and yet we hear of
'sacerdotalism' as if it were the Black Death or a
plague of Egypt, or a pestilence which walks
in darkness. In the public newspapers men are
warned, and hopes are expressed that the world
at last may be saved from 'sacerdotalism.' In the
fourth chapter of St. Paul's Epistle to the Ephe-
sians, we read these words: 'He led captivity
captive, He gave gifts to men,' 'and He gave some
apostles, and some prophets, and other some evangelists, and other some pastors and doctors (or
teachers), for the perfecting of the saints, for the
work of the ministry, for the edifying of the body of
Christ.'[15] Here is the priesthood: a body of men
chosen first by our Lord, illuminated, trained, and
conformed to Himself, to be the guardians and the
transmitters of the truths which He revealed to
them, and of the laws which He gave into their
custody. They were charged afterwards to deliver the same to others whom they should select,

[15] Eph. iv. 8, 11, 12.

whom they, in turn, should illuminate and train
to the same likeness, thereby transmitting to the
end of the world, undiminished, the custody of
Divine truth which was delivered to their charge.
This, then, is the priesthood; and there is no doubt
that it must be an object of special animosity;
and for the very reason with which I began: 'If
the world hate you, know ye that it hath hated Me
before you.' This was said to the first priests.
'If you had been of the world, the world would
love its own; but because you are not of the world,
but I have chosen you out of the world, therefore
the world hateth you.'[16] They are witnesses of
the truth, and they have power to deliver it;
and they have power to deliver it, because they
have a Divine certainty of the truth they deliver; and they have a Divine certainty of that
truth, because they are the disciples of the
Church which is divinely guided, before they become the teachers of the faithful. To them is committed the power of applying that truth to men
—that is, of guiding their thoughts and consciences, and of distinguishing truth from falsehood
in matters of faith, of judging the actions of men,

[16] St. John xv. 18, 19.

of distinguishing between right and wrong in questions of the Divine law, and of pronouncing upon them censure, if need be; giving or withholding absolution by their sentence before God. I do not wonder, therefore, that there should be an animosity in those that do not love the Master, from whose side the priesthood springs; and I do not wonder that a bad priest—if he can be found—is the hero and the saint of the world. And it never happens that an unhappy priest, either by loss of faith or by loss of fidelity, falls from his sacred state, but he is straightway glorified as a theologian, preacher, doctor, and I know not what besides. The world receives him as its own, and because he is its own, loves him.

5. Lastly, there is one person upon whom this Antichristian spirit concentrates itself, as the lightning on the conductor. There is one person upon earth who is the pinnacle of the temple, which is always the first to be struck. It is the Vicar of Jesus Christ; and that for the most obvious of reasons. There is no man on earth so near to Jesus Christ as His own Vicar. Two hundred and fifty-seven links, and we arrive at the Person of the Son of God. Two hundred and fifty-seven Pon-

K

tiffs, and we are in the presence of the Master whom His Vicar represents. That chain runs through the ages of Christian history, and connects us with the day when, on the coasts of Decapolis, Jesus said to Peter, 'Thou art Peter, and upon this rock I will build My Church, and the gates of hell shall not prevail against it.' No man therefore brings us so near to the Person of the Son of God as His Vicar upon earth, and no man is to be made so like to Him in suffering for His sake. The first nine-and-twenty Pontiffs were crowned with martyrdom. Five-and-forty times, since then, the Pontiffs have either been driven out of Rome by violence, or by violence have been hindered from setting their foot in it. Their lives have been lives of wandering, like those the Apostle describes in the Epistle to the Hebrews: 'Of whom the world was not worthy; wandering in deserts, in mountains, and in dens, and in caves of the earth.'[17] Their whole life has been a life of the Cross, and that because they bear the office, and stand in the place, of their Divine Master. The Evangelists write of Jesus, and those that were with Him; as in the Book of Acts it is Peter, and

[17] Heb. xi. 38.

those that were with him. He had taken his Master's place. And to Peter were given the two great prerogatives which constituted the plenitude of his Master's office. To him first, and to him alone, before all the others, though in the presence of the others, was given the power of the keys. To him, and to him alone, and in the presence of the others, was given also the charge of the universal flock: 'Feed My sheep.' To him, and to him alone, exclusively, were spoken the words, 'Simon, Simon, behold, Satan hath desired to have you, that he might sift you as wheat' (that is, all the Apostles); 'but I have prayed for thee' —in the singular number: for thee, Peter—'that thy faith fail not; and thou being once converted, confirm thy brethren;'[18] and therefore the plenitude of jurisdiction, and the plenitude of truth, with the 'promise of Divine assistance to preserve him in that truth, was given to Peter, and in Peter to his successors.

Compare together Rome and Constantinople. Rome, at all times assailed by a warfare so manifold that the world has hurled upon it every weapon that man could forge or direct;

[18] St. Luke xxii. 31, 32.

Constantinople, under imperial protection, fostered and endowed, sank into schism, and is in bondage to the false prophet. Rome suffering, but free; free and royal; royal and reigning over the Christian world. Make another contrast. Poor Ireland, with its unbroken tradition of immaculate Catholic Faith. Poor Ireland—what preserved it three hundred years ago, and during three hundred years of suffering for the Faith? Fidelity to the Vicar of Jesus Christ, fidelity to Rome, fidelity to the changeless See of Peter. The arch of the Faith is kept fast by that keystone, which the world would fain strike out if it could, but never has prevailed to do so; and Ireland has been sustained by it: and to this day among the nations of the Christian world there is not to be found a people so instinct with faith and so governed by Christian morality as the people of Ireland. Driven abroad into all the nations of the world, into the colonies of the British Empire, into the great northern continent of America—wheresoever they go they carry with them their faith, and sow it broadcast in works of a magnitude and generosity which we here, in the midst of all our wealth, cannot attempt to imitate. Compare with poor Ireland imperial and prosperous England. The picture would be too sad; and, as I have said before, I refrain from all that could needlessly wound any that are not of my flock. You know the past divisions and estrangements, the animosities which, I hope, are now slackened, the contentions which, I trust, are now at an end. But what a history has been the religious history of England for the last three hundred years! What is its religious state now? What will be its future? The majestic cathedrals of England, the noble abbeys, the churches of ten thousand parishes, the lofty structures of our ancient towns, the sweeter, if humbler, churches in our green hamlets, and in our woodlands, and on our solitary downs show that Faith had penetrated everywhere through the English people, and that the people were profoundly Christian. I have been reading lately the books of piety written here in England some two hundred years before what men call the Reformation, in which, if the tracing of the Spirit of God in the human heart, transcribing itself upon the page, can anywhere be found, it is in the revelations of Divine love and the interior consciousness of the soul which are left to us by our ancestors. Are Eng-

lishmen never any more to return to the unity of
the Faith? Are we never again to worship at
one altar? Are Englishmen to be united in everything but faith, and in faith to be for ever
divided? God forbid! I rejoice to know that the
English people believe profoundly in God; that,
as yet, the plague of Atheism has not made its
havoc amongst them. They believe, too, in Christianity as a Divine revelation, and therefore they
believe in Jesus Christ their Saviour; and 'no
man can say, the Lord Jesus, but by the Holy
Ghost,'[19] and 'every spirit which confesses that
Jesus Christ is come in the flesh, is of God.'[20] They
believe, too, that Holy Scripture is the written
word of God. It is true, there are to be found
here and there rationalists and critics and sceptics
and shallow heads, who may have rejected the
written word of God : but these are not the English
people. They hold it fast as their birthright. I
rejoice to know it. Ay, more than this; they have
declared themselves in these last years, and will all
the more inflexibly declare themselves, to be Christians, being sharply warned and taught by what is
now before our eyes. They will demand that their

[19] 1 Cor. xii. 3.   [20] 1 St. John iv. 2.

children too shall be brought up as Christians. I
rejoice to know all this. May God strengthen
those things that remain! May He preserve them
where they exist, and revive them where they are
declining! May He once more unite what is
divided, in the charity of truth!

Let us now sum up what has been said of the
four great evils of the day. First, we have seen that
one great evil of this day is the revolt of the intellect from God. I pointed out to you how that revolt
manifested itself in Atheism, in Deism, in heresy, in
the diminishing and explaining away of Christian
doctrine, and in practical unbelief. Secondly, I
showed you the revolt of the will from the law
of God. I traced it out in the lawlessness which
is characteristic of these later days, in the world-
worship which is a moral apostasy from God, in
the luxury which is eating out the heart of morals,
in the sensuous piety which paralyses and taints
even the devout, and in the softness and self-in-
dulgence which makes us unworthy of the Cross.
Thirdly, I endeavoured to sketch out the revolt
of society from the authority of God. I pointed
out that civil society is a Divine creation in the
order of nature; that God elevated and conse-

crated the order of nature and of politics by in-
stituting His Church in the world, and by uniting
the authority of civil government with the Christian authority of the Church. I traced out also
the rebellion, the divorce, the separation, which
has taken place between these two divine crea-
tions—the State, as it is called, and the Church—
and as a consequence, the desecration of the civil
power, the stripping of the civil society of the
world of its Christian character, and the reducing
it once more to the mere state of nature. In
those ages when society was Christian, the public
opinion, public laws, public axioms, the influence
all around, sustained the individual, raised him
upwards, and supported him in his higher life.
Now it is society that drags the individual down;
Christianity lingers in individuals, but it has
departed from society. And, lastly, I have endeavoured to draw out what the Antichristian
spirit is. It is the spirit of the world, which has
separated itself altogether from the Church and
from Christianity, or retains only a fragmentary
Christianity, and is, sometimes consciously, sometimes unconsciously, penetrated by the Antichristian enmity. I have marked also the special

objects against which this spirit directs itself: Revelation, the Catholic and Roman Church, the life of perfection, the priesthood, and the Vicar of Jesus Christ.

The general conclusion from all that I have said is this: there is no hope for man or for society but in returning to God. There is no other hope. There is nothing but God on which the soul can rest, on which society can stand. The most perfect legislation, the most refined human laws, the most acute human philosophy, political economy, benevolence, and beneficence in all its forms, all the social sciences of which we hear so much—all these are powerless without God. The most finished time-piece, in which every minute articulation is complete and perfect, cannot strike one note or measure one moment unless a living hand communicate to it the fund of motion which it afterwards exhausts. The mightiest machine which will lift a hammer of surpassing weight, break bars of iron, or cut them as if they were the branches of the fir-tree, the most wonderful structures of mechanical skill, are nothing until the momentum is given, and that momentum must be sought elsewhere. Mechanics can do nothing without dynamical powers; and these dynamical powers, for men and for society, are to be found in God alone. They can be found only in Him to whose image man is made; they can be found nowhere but in His truth, which is the key of the human intellect, and in His grace, which is the only hand that can touch the heart in man; and if this be so, they can be found only in Christianity. Neither adults nor children can be touched by the laws of states, except externally. The state may control the external actions of men—it can imprison, it can fine, it can inflict capital punishment; but it cannot convert the sinner, nor change the will, nor illuminate the intellect, nor guide the conscience, nor shape a character. It cannot educate a child. All this is internal, not external; it is not mechanism; it belongs to the living powers of the soul; and God alone, by truth and grace, can accomplish this work in man.

I implore you, in God's name, and all the more because of the events, full of sorrow and of shame to Christian men, which have crowded so thick upon us in these last months, I may say in this last week, that, with all your heart and will, and all the weight of your soul, you cast yourselves on

God. He alone can save. Use all your influence with those around you, in your homes, your households, your friendships; and if you have public influence, public trust, public authority, strive that all who bear responsibility shall cast themselves on God, as the only hope for society and for the people. Do you want to see what man without God can do? Read the history of the last eighty years in Paris. You have there one simple phenomenon—generation rising after generation without God in the world. And why? Because without Christian education. First, an atheistical revolution; next, an empire penetrated through and through with a mocking philosophy and a reckless indifferentism; afterwards came Governments, changed in name and in form, but not in practice nor in spirit. The Church, trammelled by protection, its spiritual action faint and paralysed, could not penetrate the masses of the people, nor form the rising youth. It laboured fervently; its sons fought nobly for Christian freedom; thousands were saved; but for eighty years the mass of men has grown up without God and without Christ in the world. My whole soul pities them. These outbursts of horror, strife, outrage, sacrilege, bloodshed, are the harvest reaped from the rank soil in which such seed was cast. All this is true. But how did souls created to the image of God grow up in such a state? They were robbed: robbed before they were born, robbed of their inheritance, and reared up in an education without Christianity. Let this be a warning to ourselves. We are on the turn of the tide. A few active, busy, confident, and eloquent men were a year ago carrying us away with theories of state education without religion. We were told that a child might be taught to read and to write and to spell and to sum without Christianity. Who denies it? But what does this make of them? To what would they grow up? The formation of the will and heart and character, the formation of a man, is education, and not the reading and the writing and the spelling and the summing. For fifteen hundred years, Christians served God and loved man, before as yet they received this cultivation; and we, because we have it profusely, we are forgetting the deeper and diviner lessons. The tradition of Christian education in England is as yet unbroken. It is threatened now for the first time. In God's name, stand fast, and save it. I can add no more. Do not be afraid, if you find yourselves in the minority. 'Wo to you when men shall bless you!'[21] You must be censured if you are the disciples of Jesus Christ. The world that hated Him will not love you. 'The disciple is not above his master, nor the servant above his lord. It is enough for the disciple that he be as his master, and the servant as his lord.'[22] 'If they have called the master of the house Beelzebub, how much more them of his household?' And therefore, if you have the mark of the world's hatred upon you, accept it; press it to your bosom. It is the token that you are the disciples of the true and only Master. If you have the world's favour and sunshine, look to yourselves. There is a dark future before the world. What it may be, God alone knows. The Church will have to suffer; but there is a light upon it, and that light can never fade. We are in evil times, marked deeply by the four great evils of which I have spoken. Around us are 'evil men and seducers, who grow worse and worse, erring, and driving into error.'[23] 'Many shall come in My name,' our Lord has said,

[21] St. Luke vi. 26.   [22] St. Matt. x. 24, 25.   [23] 2 Tim. iii. 14.

'and seduce many;' and because of their iniquity the love and the charity of the many shall wax cold. Nation shall rise against nation, and kingdom against kingdom; and there shall be wars and pestilences in many places. But the end is not yet. This is only the beginning of troubles. Keep close to the footsteps of the Master who spoke those words; and, when these signs are in the sky and upon the earth, remember that He also said, 'When these things begin to come to pass, look up, and lift up your heads; for your redemption is at hand.'[24]

[24] St. Luke xxi. 28.

.

THE END.

LONDON:

ROBSON AND SONS, PRINTERS, PANCRAS ROAD, N.W.

www.ingramcontent.com/pod-product-compliance
Lightning Source LLC
Chambersburg PA
CBHW021133020726
47500CB00003B/1060